I0626463

THE RAVAGER
ALAN SPENCER

Severed Press
Hobart Tasmania

THE RAVAGER

Copyright © 2015 Alan Spencer
Copyright © 2015 by Severed Press

www.severedpress.com

All rights reserved. No part of this book may be
reproduced or transmitted in any form or by any
electronic or mechanical means, including
photocopying, recording or by any information and
retrieval system, without the written permission of
the publisher and author, except where permitted by
law.
This novel is a work of fiction. Names,
characters, places and incidents are the product of
the author's imagination, or are used fictitiously.
Any resemblance to actual events, locales or persons,
living or dead, is purely coincidental.

ISBN: 978-1-925225-95-2

All rights reserved.

Chopper Dan

This is the easiest paycheck ever, Chopper Dan kept thinking. *I sit here smoking my cigars, picking my butt, and watching people blow up shit. Fuck News Channel Five. Canning my ass was the best thing they could ever do to me. 'Chopper Dan here. It's five o'clock in the morning right now. I had to get up at three just to make it to work on time. That's way too early for any sane man to open up his eyes. Oh well, half-awake guy in a chopper reporting for morning duty. I'm up in the sky in my big bird, so you better watch out, because I plan on taking a big shit on your heads. Wake up, Se-attle!'*

Chopper Dan sat in the back of his parked helicopter waiting for the five-person crew to finish their job. Robert Prager had hired the pilot to deliver them to Chichi-Hama Island. The island exists as one among many islands on the Pacific Ocean. The fact the island has no local natives made it all the easier for Robert and his team to do their job.

Their job? Blasting for gold.

It's what I do for a living, Chopper Dan remembered the boisterous Robert Prager telling him over the phone. *I've sent two girls and two boys to college, and supported three different wives on what I make. I know gold. It's in my veins, and keep in mind, if I don't find a speck of gold on the island, you still get paid. I won't ask about how you lost your job at News Channel Five. How much better does it get?*

Chopper Dan didn't like talking about how he got sacked from his news job. It was a struggle making ends meet after his termination, until he realized how famous he was because of his unusual reason for being fired. He became a kind of character the public embraced, a viral sensation.   His new trade was flying tourists in his helicopter inside the Grand Canyon and The Red Desert. Now, Dan was branching out. He was taking random gigs from people like Robert Prager, who needed transport on special jobs.

Robert paid well.

Really, really well.

Chopper Dan could relax, enjoy the downtime, and stack the greenbacks.

Two hours passed before the giant rock face on the east blew up. One boom. Two booms. Three booms. Eight more booms. The pounding of dynamite was very loud, even from Dan's far out position. The rock face was reduced to a wall of white dust and tumbling boulders.

"Boom Bitch!" Robert called out to Chopper Dan through his walkie. "There's gold in 'dem dere hills! My wife needs a new face, and a new set of tits. Come on, gimme some gold! Put it in my hands, and I'll take it to the bank."

Chopper Dan eyed the crew at work through his binoculars. The crew wore gas masks and climbing gear. They approached the broken up rock face. A giant hole had formed, thanks to the dynamite. They were entering a deep cave-like entrance. He easily assumed this was where the gold was hidden.

Dan brought a book with him. The team would excavate, dig, and search for those valuable nuggets for who knew how long. They had food and rations for three days. Dan had a lot of time to kill before the job was done.

Fifty pages into his paperback, he heard a fast series of blasts.

Boom-da-boom-da-boom-da-boom-da-boom.

Chopper Dan wasn't sure if it was a scheduled blast, until Robert whooped into the walkie, "BOOM BITCH! We're going in deeper. We've found evidence there's gold in this place, and lots of it. Everybody is going to be stinkin' rich. You're getting a raise, Dan. If this takes longer than scheduled, I'll double your pay. You just make sure that bird is ready to fly the coop when we're done."

Chopper Dan dug out his silver flask from his vest pocket and enjoyed a pull. He reported back, "I got my end of the job handled. No worries, pal. So blast away. Stack up your gold. You'll fill up Fort Knox before you know it."

The sun was starting to get brighter. They arrived on the island at the breaking of dawn, and now, it was high noon. Chopper Dan was swatting at random exotic-looking bugs and wiping rolling beads of sweat from his face. If he was hot, he could only imagine how the team was holding up.

I've got all the shade and bottled water a man could ever need. Bring it on.

Chopper Dan had fallen asleep inside the helicopter, bored out of his mind, when the ground started to rumble. This wasn't a dynamite blast. The ground vibrated for minutes on end, and it hadn't stopped. The whole island seemed to be shifting. He imagined a giant rock shelf rubbing against another rock shelf.

Grrrrrrrrrrrrrrrrrrrrrrrrrrrrrrrrrrrrrraaaaaaaaaah!

Something enormous growled. He imagined a rabid dog mixed with a high-pitched bat shriek. So loud, Chopper Dan cupped his ears.

"Have that chopper ready, Dan! It's coming for us!"

Robert's voice was heavy with fear. The jovial, overconfident man had been downgraded to a terrorized idiot.

Chopper Dan wanted to demand what was coming after them. No matter how many times he called them on the walkie, the team wouldn't answer.

I knew this job was too easy.

Something had to happen.

Damn it all anyway!

He worked to start up the chopper when the entire rock face the team had excavated burst, as if punched through from the other side. What shot forth was so huge, so magnificent that Chopper Dan couldn't take in the enormity. It wasn't human, nor was it animal. Beast. Monstrosity. Creature. Behemoth. Juggernaut. Those were words that fit the bill.

Chopper Dan's mouth gaped open at the bulk. The enormity was easily the size of a giant skyscraper. The creature reared its head back and screeched.

Raaaaaaaaaaaaaaaaaaaaaaaaaaaaatch!

Chopper Dan reeled at the living marvel through his binoculars. He searched the broken up hill for any signs of the team. Seconds later, he spotted Robert and the others. They were on top of the hill, staying still, and by their expressions, praying the monster didn't locate them.

He caught small glimpses of the horrific monster. The monster's black-plated back tinged gold when the sun caught it dead on. Its long and thick tail swept through a clearing of trees and rendered them into smithereens with one single lashing. Those giant oblong eyes took up half of its head. They were black with fiery red circles in the middle. He imagined a lizard on steroids, followed up by an injection of primordial rage. Its jagged, plated chest kept inhaling and exhaling hard, as if about to unleash another deadly fit.

Robert and the group were making a break for it.

No, it'll see you! Stay where you're at. Hide. Damn it, you can't run!

The group sprinted from behind a pile of displaced boulders. They were stomping down the hill and onto the path that led back to the helicopter. They had at least a half of a mile to cover before they would reach Chopper Dan's location. Fear had driven them to take the chance, not intellect, and they would pay the hefty price of ignorance.

The beast turned its bulk around and rampaged towards them.

Chopper Dan watched in horror through the binoculars and what unfolded next.

The team kept running like hell.

It didn't matter.

The beast lowered its body so it was on all fours, posed like a lizard. Then it unleashed the loudest shriek. Dan only caught a brief glimpse of the damage before cupping his ears and shutting his eyes in pain.

The screech was so loud, so high-pitched, that the air rushing out of its mouth was a powerful blast of force. Robert and his team were de-fleshed by the sound waves. They were standing there one moment, and the next, they were screaming bloody skeletons just before the monster raised its monstrous calls to a new octave, and rendered them into super sonic smashed vapor.

The monster was stomping right for Chopper Dan now. Its hamburger jowls were drooling God knows what. He could see that when the drool hit the trees, they fizzed and evaporated. Acid eaten.

He had to think fast. Running and hiding wasn't enough to guarantee survival.

You're dead if you don't think of something.

This ain't like reporting the morning weather.

Chopper Dan didn't have enough time to rev up the helicopter and high fly it out of there. He thought of the next best thing.

Robert had left a box of dynamite in the chopper. The pilot grabbed as many individuals sticks as he could, dug out his lighter, and took off running.

Raaaaaaaaaaaaaaaaaaaaaaaaaaaaatch!

He was nearly taken off his feet by the way everything was rocked by the beast's angry call.

Chopper Dan lit a stick and threw it up at the angry monster. The dynamite went boom at its feet. It did absolutely nothing.

Charging faster through the woods, he lit another stick, the fuse burning lightning-fast, and BOOM BITCH.

This one exploded higher up its legs.

Graaaaaaaaaaaagh! Gr-aaaaaaaaaaaaagh!

The thing was pissed. Razor-tipped claws slashed at trees and vegetation. Chopper Dan realized he was the mouse, and this monster was the eagle baring down on him. Any second, he'd be gobbled up. He imagined himself being squished between a set of teeth, and turned over on a tongue, until that horrible saliva melted him down. How long would he feel the agony before he died?

He decided that he didn't want to find out, and lit yet another stick of dynamite. He turned, launched the dynamite really high, and the stick went off at the beast's chest. The monster paused, staggered back two steps, and right when he thought he might have a chance, the beast was rearing back its head again.

No, you don't! I'm not letting you scream the skin off of me!

Chopper Dan realized he only had one stick of dynamite left.

"Fucking fuck you!"

He lit the fuse, tensed his arm, took aim, and with everything left in his body, Chopper Dan released his own version of hell, fastball style. Everything transpired in slow motion as the stick spun from top to bottom repeatedly. When the explosion occurred, the monster seemed to be in pain. It retreated, screeching and wailing.

I see. That's what you don't like!

Very interesting, you giant bitch.

Before Chopper Dan could do anything else, the retreating monster's tail smashed through the trees surrounding him. He ducked and dodged the hailstorm of flying wood. He thought a tornado was sweeping through the area.

Chopper Dan's legs were striding through empty air before he could process what had forced him off his feet. He flipped three times. When he struck the ground, it was lights out.

Nick Folder

I could be any one of these people in Las Vegas, as long as I got the money and the urge to spend it. I can be the family man with the screaming brats. The frat boy who wants to get laid. I could be the grease ball who wants to buy a hooker from those cheap laborers waving those pulpy fliers on the sidewalks of Vegas. 'Get your pussy here. All flavors, colors, and shapes. Whatever you're into, it's only a phone call away. Perfectly legal!'

Pick any vice.

Nobody will stop you, as long as you got the green.

I got the money, and I get to be anybody I want to be. I can stay at Caesar's Palace, The Riviera, The Mirage, Bally's, The Luxor, or the Palazzo, but today, where I stay, how I spend my money, and who I sleep with, is up to me.

Nobody controls me ever again.

I'm just an average guy. I'm not the man who can't keep track of the number of people he's killed. I don't have to have a conscience that's blacker than the tarmac lining the cities of hell. I can be the person I was before the United States turned me into something nobody should ever become. I don't have to close my eyes at night and know my dreams will be painted in blood red.

As long as one person thinks I'm the old me, the me before matters of national security turned me into a murderer, that's all I need to enjoy my vacation. I don't mind pretending to be someone I'm not. I'm Joe Nobody, and thank you very much for calling me that.

Thank God for you, Audra Merrit.

Without that woman, I wouldn't have a reason to be myself again.

Nick Folder had just got off the plane from The Middle East. He took a cab straight to his hotel, The Bitterwell Casino. It was the tallest building in Las Vegas. It was also the newest hotel and casino on the famous strip. Billboards bragged that this casino had three times the number of slot machines and gaming tables than its competition. The place was a giant glass monolith with gold trim. It eclipsed its neighbors in its shadow. If you viewed an aerial shot, The Bitterwell Casino stood the proudest of all the buildings on the Las Vegas strip, no competition.

The front circular parking area featured pieces of post-modern art. Nick couldn't tell the beginning and end of them. They were like abstract versions of men and women, all cast in gold, and pointing at the sky. What they were pointing at, only God could tell you, and maybe even God couldn't tell you what it all meant.

Nick tipped the taxi driver and carried his single travel bag into The Bitterwell Casino. He was in plainclothes. He was shaggy in appearance, sunburned, with a long overgrown beard, and his wild black hair was down to his shoulders.

You look just like a terrorist, so you might want to consider making yourself over before meeting your friend. You've been playing in the sand too long, Nick. It's been awhile since you've come up for air. I'm just saying, Nick, as your advisor...a shave won't kill you, especially for the lady's sake.

His superior, Donovan Hewitt, was full of advice, right before Nick was released for his vacation. Could the man also tell Nick what to do about his nightmares and memories?

Hell no.

So I'm stuck with getting a makeover. That'll dry the blood from my hands and wipe clean the high body count I've accumulated over the years.

Yeah. R-ight.

At least my nails will look nice, and I'll smell like a movie star.

Nick checked in at the front desk. The government wasn't holding back. He had the King's Suit. Nick could only imagine what lavish excesses were in that room. Movie stars could afford these places, not deep undercover government goons in their early forties.

Nick ran through his script again, for when he met up with his ex-girlfriend from high school, Audra Merrit.

I'm Nick Carter. Insurance claims agent. A man with money to burn. I'm a fun-loving son-of-a-bitch, not a man on the verge of a psychotic breakdown. Who's on the verge of losing his shit? Not me. I'm in Vegas, baby. I'll put my money on black.

Try to have a good time, Nick, Donovan Hewitt advised him before his vacation was approved. *If you're still having your troubles, we'll deal with those when you come back to work. Some rest and relaxation cures even the most...tired of men. You're meeting up with your old flame. If rest and relaxation can cure a man of most anything, so can a night with a wild woman. Get laid. Trust me, Nick. Cleaning your pipes will cleanse your soul. It's like rebooting your computer.*

Nick knew he wasn't going to get better because of a short vacation and getting his dick wet. He was smarter than the military gave him credit for.

You just made a mistake, because I'm not coming back. I'll enjoy this vacation. I'll play along. Then you'll never hear from me again. I'm done being used and exploited. If it weren't for my parents being killed in Afghanistan--

"Excuse me, sir, are you okay?"

Nick wasn't sure how he ended up sitting in a chair in the front lobby. He was so lost in his thoughts that it took him several moments to realize he had a hotel key in his hand, and an agonized expression playing on his face.

The hotel attendant, a sweet older Asian woman, gave him a nervous smile. "Sir, how may I accommodate you? Can I get you a drink? May we help you to your room?"

Nick had to clear his throat, so he wouldn't sound so distressed. "I guess I'm a bit overwhelmed by all of this. I don't know where to start. I'm overdue for a vacation. Stress. You know how it is." *Don't tell them who you really are.* "I work in insurance, and the hours are grueling. I've done so well that my job has given me an all-expenses paid package."

"Oh sir, that's wonderful," the attendant said. "Here, let me have one of our bellhops take your suitcase. Let's get you taken care of. Now what sounds fun to you?"

The lady, at least fifty years old, and arms so skinny that Nick thought she could easily break, asked, "Any plans, besides gambling?"

"I'm meeting an old friend later. A real nice lady."

"I see," the woman gave a strange laugh. "How about a stop at our spa? We'll give you the five-start treatment, sir. Real good. We'll have you looking real sharp. Pretty girl won't know what hit her."

Nick didn't care. Money wasn't an issue. He looked like hell. Maybe the spa could erase some of the grit off his face. They would need a jackhammer. Nick prayed whoever shaved his face had a sharp enough razor.

He let it all happen. No questions. Nick kept saying yes to every package option. The Asian lady had him by the arm, and she was guiding him into the spa with square glass bricks for walls. Over a dozen people had worked him over in the coming two hours. Twelve hundred dollars later, he had undergone a full body massage, hot bamboo massage, exfoliating cleanse, manicure, pedicure, shave, and a haircut from a flamboyant girl who chewed the fruitiest smelling gum. "Darling" convinced him to dye his hair from black to blond. "It'll put the sunshine back into your face. Look, you're smiling already. Don't hide it. Keep smiling, you lady killer."

He did smile.

The way the woman had cut his hair, he looked like a California surfer dude who had just formed a mega kick-starter company.

When Nick presented his credit card to pay at the front desk, the cashier, a tall brunette in her late thirties, gave him a double look.

"Wow, Mr. Folder. You look great, amazing what a bit of pampering does for a man. Guys need to enjoy these services as much as women do. I'm glad you came in, Mr. Folder."

"Call me Nick."

On his way out of the spa, he eyed himself in a mirror. His hard-lined face, droopy eyes, and young haggard face had done a real one-eighty.

For the first time in years, he felt okay with himself.

Maybe pretending to be happy isn't so overrated.

Right when Nick made his way back into the lobby, a big man in a silver suit approached him. The guy had the esteem of a rich businessman. His belly threatened to break free from his tightly buttoned suit. Two cigars poked out from his front pocket. He reeked of a freshly smoked Havana. The dark, orange-tanned stranger introduced himself as "the" Heath Bitterwell.

Heath shook Nick's hand. "Welcome to The Bitterwell Casino. I built this place after almost a decade of fundraising and planning. Can't say it didn't go without a hitch. Buildings in Vegas don't cost a dime. She's quite the beauty. I'm glad our staff helped to accommodate you. You look like a million bucks, Mr. Folder."

Nick was about to ask Heath how he knew his name, when the boisterous butterball told him how. "I got a memo this morning from a very private sector of government. This doesn't happen everyday. Never, actually. I know about your service to our great country. People like you make our freedom possible. Allow me the honor to invite you to enjoy any of our many fine accommodations, on the house.

"I see you've already made reservations to meet an Audra Merrit at our steakhouse. Consider her bill on the house too. It's been prearranged, and let me assure you, nothing, and I mean nothing, will prevent you from having a good time. I stake my reputation on it."

Nick was put off by the intensity of Heath Bitterwell's eyes. There was a certain zeal that didn't belong in a man's eyes when talking about a building. They belonged to a butcher who enjoyed the slaughter.

"Thank you, Mr. Bitterwell. You have a fine hotel and casino. That's why I picked it out. It's the best on the block."

"Good to hear," Mr. Bitterwell said. "Now, I'll see that someone escorts you to your room so you can settle in. Please, if you need anything, here's my private line. Anything you need, I'll take care of it."

Mr. Bitterwell handed Nick his business card.

The man's hands were shaking. There was sweat beading on Mr. Bitterwell's forehead.

Strange, Nick thought, *why is this man so nervous?*

Nick accepted the card, thanked the man, and waited for the bellboy to take him up to his room.

Heath Bitterwell

Heath Bitterwell couldn't get a read on Nick Folder. Mr. Folder was soft-spoken and humble, but that quiet intensity in his eyes, said that Nick was up to something. A man like Nick was capable of infiltrating the casino operation. Two years of business, and nobody was onto Heath Bitterwell. It couldn't last forever, he thought, but why now? Why Nick Folder? The tax papers, the legalities, the secrecy, the engineering, the sadistic creativity, everything was crafted to be legit and hush hush. Heath had a lot of excellent people on his payroll to ensure that the casino's extra affairs stayed unknown.

However, today, the Bitterwell was hit with the biggest red flag. Why would he get a call from the Secretary of Defense to treat Nick Folder like a movie star? Who is this Nick Folder, and what kind of game was the government playing with him?

They're onto me.

They know what I had to do to have this building built.

They know about my operations.

They fucking know everything, and they're going to spring the trap on me. Nick Folder is a triggerman. I'll be dead by the end of the night.

Heath retreated to an employee's only door after having that short talk with Nick. He was out-of-breath and sweating through his suit. He clutched his chest, thinking his heart would explode. Heath removed his suit jacket, and raced to a service elevator.

This was a special elevator. It was a normal elevator, but whenever Heath spoke, a voice-activated system allowed the elevator to take him up to the core of The Bitterwell Casino. Nobody else had access to this part of the building.

The secret place of operations.

I don't care who is here.

Nobody will find out.

If they do, I'll fight back.
They'll regret ever digging too deep into my affairs.
I'll make them pay.
They won't take me in alive.

The elevator stopped on the thirty-fourth floor. Head of security, Sid Rigard, a tall thug in a black suit, an ex-prize fighter, and an ugly tough guy who had the face of a bulldog, met Heath at the elevator.

"What's the word on Nick Folder?"

"Nothing just yet," Heath said. "He's got me worried. I don't like the way I'm feeling."

"What can I do, sir?"

"Keep tabs on this Nick Folder. Make sure he doesn't do anything suspicious. He could be a spy, FBI, DEA, or God knows what. It scares me to think of what he's up to."

"You want me to take him out for you?" Sid smiled, and clenched his fists. His breathing had increased. The man's thick tongue wet his lips. The bulldog was hungry. "I'll kill him any way you like. I'll even it do it in front of a security camera so you can watch. Give me the order, sir. I'll snap his neck. I'll strangle him until his eyes pop out of his head. I'll cave in his face. I'll stomp his skull in. I'll exploit every pressure point until he confesses everything to me. Anything you fancy, sir, I'll make it happen. You know I'll deliver."

"I need a drink," Heath said, gasping for air. His heart was chugging as if he'd run a marathon and lard was blocking up his arteries. Any more stress, and POP, he'd tear an aorta and croak. "I need a drink, *now.*"

Sid snapped his fingers. Seconds later, what Heath called his "cocktail girls," hurried to his location. One was a former Miss America from five years ago who had gone from crown to cock, when she became a porn star. Now, she was Heath's full-time cocktail girl. She was a blonde bombshell who paraded around in a pair of red silk panties, topless, and in black high heels. Heath liked "Melissa" because she had the whitest skin and the pinkest nipples, and those D-cups were very much real. Heath's hands knew all.

Melissa carried a tray with three highball glasses of high-end bourbon. Heath threw back two of them, and then Melissa soothed him. "Put your head on my chest, Heathy baby. I know how to make you feel better. Anything for my Heathy baby. Go ahead; rest your head on my pillows."

Heath had no problem doing as he was told.

She had the softest pillows.

A six-girl team of cocktail girls were now standing in the ranks, each clad, or not so clad, in a variety of lingerie and sexy attire. They helped soothe Heath in his moment of distress.

After lifting his head from Melissa's chest, Heath regarded the line of women. He liked to put his girlies in compartments. Sleazy. All-American. Goth. Exotic. Forbidden. Debutantes. Healthy. His women were all of those things, and more, and Heath was starting to feel the rhythm of his heart return to normal.

"Thank you, ladies," Heath said. "Later tonight, you can do me another favor, all of you."

The women giggled, laughed, blushed, bounced in place enough to make their tits jiggle, and generally played along with the rich guy's fantasy. They had to, Heath thought, because they were being paid, and that meant Heath had the power to realize any dreams he could muster. He had The Bitterwell Casino, and that made him the most powerful person in the city, maybe even in the country.

The cocktail girls returned to the workstations, a waiting room where they waited on-call to meet Heath's needs. Sid stood there waiting, eyeing the women's assets as they strutted away.

"I'm glad you're feeling better, sir," Sid said. "Now about this Nick Folder."

"I know what to do. Consider us on high alert until Nick Folder's stay here is finished."

"Why not just kill him?"

"Because we don't know for sure why he's here. It might even be nothing. I want to wait this out a bit, and feel this son-of-a-bitch out, before we do anything rash and irreversible."

Heath led Sid down a blank hallway. When they reached the end, Heath stopped at a steel door. There was both a key code password and a voice-activated password that allowed him access. Heath entered both, and the vault door opened. After Sid closed it behind them, they entered a short hallway. They completed the short walk to the next thick steel door with three more security codes. Entering this room, there were thousands of bank lock boxes lining both walls. Hundreds of stashes of money, weapons, evidence, private files, documents, and anything you could fit in a square of steel surrounded them. Billions and billions of dollars were stored here under safekeeping. Hundreds of crimes were kept secret within these thick walls.

Heath wasn't focused on the money.

Security was what mattered.

This was his job, and Heath had to come through, or else it'd be his head on a platter one day. The Mexican Cartels. The Juarez Cartel. The Chinese Cartel. The Tokyo Cartel. The Russian Cartel. The overseas syndicates. This place was a hideaway, bank, and haven for these criminals, and it was Heath's job to protect everything. There was only one comfort when the government, or anyone, threatened his secret operation.

Heath and Sid stood in front of the final door in the passage.

The War Room.

Nobody, and I mean nobody, will ever threaten me in anyway. They have no idea what this building is capable of. Only I do.

Heath and Sid entered the War Room.

They had some work to do.

Ray Desanti

Ray Desanti sweated in the unmarked black van parked down the block from The Bitterwell Casino. Ray studied the shining Mecca of glass and gold. Ray could wipe his ass with all of it. Money and the high life were useless things when everybody you loved was dead.

The contemplative man used a rag to wipe his pale, bald, head, shaved so close to the skin that not even a single bud of hair showed. Ray chugged hard on his bottle of water. He'd prefer something harder, but the heat, and tonight's job, both required his faculties.

This was going to be one hell of a night, Ray kept telling himself. Every time he reminded himself, Ray couldn't hold back the evil smile from spreading across his intense face. He was ready to deliver hell to The Bitterwell Casino.

You can kill a man's family, Desanti thought, you can take away his livelihood, and you can leave him bleeding in the desert with four bullets lodged deep in his stomach. However, if you don't make sure he's dead, and dead for good, there will always be a reason for even the most dejected and hopeless man to live on.

That reason to live on?

Revenge.

Ray used to be a drug mule between the Mexico and Arizona border before his near death experience. Anything from cocaine, heroin, and marijuana, he found inventive ways of stashing the items on his person without being caught. Even the drug dogs couldn't catch him in the act. The problem, Ray's father loved to gamble. Dice and black jack were his supreme vices. He played with over a dozen big cartel boys, like Ribald, Stiff, Hammer, Crusher, Baggs, Knuckles, Spider, Red Panda, and Spreader.

Ray's father had accumulated so many debts between so many bad people that, one day Ray's father was buried neck-deep in the Red Desert. Five people bashing in his skull with baseball bats beat the man to death. The bright sun exposed every smashed piece of meat and bone in vivid colors. His father's death was on a permanent loop deep in Ray's shattered subconscious.

Ray's two sisters, his mother, his only brother, and four of his cousins witnessed the savage beating. Afterward, the rest of Ray's family was shot dead on sight. The cartels members made an event of it. Between executing each of them, they shared drinks, cartel stories, and how Ray's father was a dumb gambling bastard who had it coming, and how they'd enjoy taking over his piece of the drug business.

Ray was the last one to be shot. The rest of his family was bleeding into the sand and he on the way to the other side well before the first bullet penetrated his stomach. Red Panda, that bitch, and Knuckles, blasted Ray with four shots to the solar plexus with their 9mms.

The cartel members left in their vehicles, leaving Ray to twitch and ooze in the desert heat. If it weren't for that random border patrol vehicle happening upon him, Ray would be dead.

You don't send a man to his grave without closing the casket first.

You bastards made one serious mistake.

You didn't kill me.

Now I'm here for payback.

Ray checked his watch.

Only a few more hours, and his plan would begin.

He knew how to hurt the cartels, more than simply executing the perpetrators. Yes, he'd do that too, because he remembered the triggermen, and they were enjoying a stay at The Bitterwell Casino today.

Ray kept track of those who came and went in The Bitterwell Casino over the course of nine months. The gangs were close, and they enjoyed that special haven The Bitterwell Casino extended to the criminals in the drug business. Every three months or so, they crashed here in Vegas to blow off steam and enjoy expensive fun.

Ray made visual confirmation of the gang's stay two days ago. They weren't leaving until the end of the week. That gave him plenty of time for revenge.

The casino would run red with blood and hot with bullets.

Execution wasn't enough. Ray would attack them where it really hurt.

Their pocketbooks.

Ray drank more of his bottled water, and checked his watch again. Only a few more hours, and the blood would start flowing.

Chopper Dan

I'm not dead!

Chopper Dan woke from brief unconsciousness with a head that felt like a pressure cooker full of bursting grenades. He wasn't bleeding from his head, but he could feel a big knot forming on the back of his skull. By the end of the day that knot would be a bulging softball.

He forced himself to snap out of it, and really access the scene. A screen of dust was settling all around him. Trees were felled, literally punched and kicked through, creating a direct path into the Pacific Ocean. Waves lapped against the shore from the great monster's plunge into the water.

Robert Prager and his team of gold diggers were dead. He had no job anymore. No paycheck either. All he had was a sore body, an angry headache, and a feeling that his life had gone from good to really fucking bad, in the amount of time it took a gigantic creature to surface from deep within the earth.

The average person would consider that black-plated beast a major scientific find. Chopper Dan had seen the way that monster had used its screams to rip skin from the human body. The beast surely had other tricks up its sleeve. The thing was a murderer. Masses of people were in danger, and Chopper Dan had to stop it.

He had to navigate his way through the woods carefully to locate his helicopter. He had to backtrack a couple of times, because he was still funny in the head.

The transport was untouched.

Maybe his luck hadn't run out.

Chopper Dan fired up the chopper, quickly going airborne. Tracking the thing would be easy, he thought. He kept following the ripples of waves on the water. Logic dictated, he would catch up with the monster eventually. Chopper Dan wasn't sure how much of a head start the big bastard had on him.

He hadn't been unconscious for very long, because the profile of the beast appeared ahead in the ocean after only a short period of time. Chopper Dan could see its oblong, lizard-shaped head. Those horrible globe eyes were enormous and frightening. They were all black, with a solid circle of blood red in the center. Demonic. Down its plated back was jagged vertebra sticking up from its skin. He imagined bone stalactites as long as buildings, and sharp as steel. The tail slashed at the water, the powerful whip lashing the surface and propelling the beast forward at incredible speeds.

Chopper Dan was about to grab his radio, and call in for help, when up from the sky, a series of B2 Bombers zipped across the sky. Aircraft carriers appeared in the waters up ahead, armed with high-tech machine guns and missiles. More attack jets were launching off the other aircraft carrier runways. Countless assault planes kept showing up on the scene.

He wasn't sure how the Navy showed up so fast, but then he realized Robert Prager's brother was a high-ranking officer in the Navy. Robert must have called for help when the beast was stalking them.

Chopper's radio went off. "Attention, you are about to enter a firing zone. You must--"

The signal was cut off when the monster surged up from the ocean and screamed so loud, the glass in Chopper Dan's helicopter cracked. He was knocked off-course, side winding, and going upside down. He couldn't right the steering wheel for several agonizing seconds. The helicopter was nothing against the blast of scream-wind.

Those fucking screams!

He retained control of the helicopter and stayed a good distance away from the monster.

Chopper tried to tell them what the monster didn't like, but his radio wasn't responding.

"Damn it, work. WORK!"

He tried, and tried again. The radio was useless. Chopper Dan had no means to fight the monster with his chopper. It was for transport only.

Chopper Dan could really hurt the monster, if he had the chance. He saw how it reacted back on the island. He knew its weakness. He lost his train of thought when the ocean suddenly became a deadly battleground. The pilot could only watch and pray that the good guys won the fight.

Nick Folder

The King's Suite was no joke. Nick had a private movie theatre in one corner of the room. He could view any one of hundreds of movies, and order anything from popcorn, soft pretzels, to pizza, and fifty other snacks. The room was also equipped with a fully stocked bar, including dozens of varieties of hard liquor and beer on tap. A smaller room in the corner acted as a humidor for fresh cigars. He imagined the fat cash someone paid to spend one night in this place.

Nick laughed at the hot tub that faced the glass wall looking on at the Vegas strip. He had a perfect view of Treasure Island, the casino across the street. Nick watched a mock battle take place, as pirates pretended to shoot each other on a life-sized pirate ship replica.

Fake violence, Nick thought. What a joke. If only the death he'd seen were only special effects. What he'd give. Even standing here in this lavish, ridiculous sweet, all he could see was death.

There was a complimentary bottle of champagne in a bucket of ice propped on the living room table. When he saw that bucket, Nick remembered the Tijuana death camp he had been taken prisoner in years ago. Members of his military unit were captured, and Nick was forced to carry the butchered remains of his fellow team members in buckets. He would lug loads of eyeballs, hands, assorted guts, and dump them into a pig trough. The hardest part of the job wasn't the smell, but when he could identify to whom the cut up pieces belonged.

The morbid associations in the room didn't stop there.

The painting up against the living room wall depicted an ocean's view of a tropical paradise. His mind distorted that imagine into something else entirely. All Nick could see were hanging slabs of human meat with hooks jammed through their backs. Nick had played dead in Baghdad when trying to infiltrate an active terrorist ring. After his 'dead' body was taken in, he was thrown in a freezer of bodies. He was placed on the floor, yet to be hung up like a dead piece of meat. Nick remembered the smells, the colors, the frigid cold, and the feeling of helplessness, and of dread, because he knew once he escaped that freezer, he was confident in his killing abilities. He murdered eleven suspected terrorists with a single meat hook and a length of chain. When military aircraft picked him up, Nick dug in his pants pocket for cigarettes, and instead of smokes, he pulled out a severed tongue.

Still, the suite kept dredging up terrible memories.

The bed shaped as a heart with its red silk cover, Nick saw lengths and lengths of human intestines gleam. He had to sleep in a pit of animal organs, deep underground, to hide from Bin Laden's gang, after he had been identified as an American spy. Two days, he waded in the offal, just to survive.

The smooth black floor of the suite reminded him of the dark slab of steel where Nick had to torture a Russian spy that was suspected of having stolen classified government files from the United States. Nick used a hot curling iron and a hammer and nails to pry the truth from the spy. It wasn't until five nails were driven through the man's scrotum skin that the Russian told all.

The worst thing in the room was that blank movie screen. Sure, it was blank, but once Nick's eyes were trained on it for more than two seconds, images began to play out on the screen. His parents, each photojournalists, were doing freelance work in Afghanistan. They brought Nick, who was nineteen at the time, along for an amazing world experience. When their plane landed, members of Al Qaeda seized the American passengers as captives. Nick didn't remember much except for the hood placed over his head that smelled like a camel's ass, and his own hot breath.

He heard his parents crying, and telling Nick they loved him, and how they were sorry this was happening. Nick couldn't put it together why they were saying these things until he heard the machete blade slice off his parents' head.

After the decapitations, someone was speaking in a foreign language.

They were videotaping the executions live on the Internet.

When he heard his mother's last words, "Nick, do something to save yourself," something within Nick changed. His mother's words flipped a switch. His fear vanished. The fact that his hands were tied behind his back, and his head was covered with a hood, didn't matter anymore. What stopped mattering was everything, because these bastards had decapitated his parents in cold blood, and recorded it for a bullshit cause.

Nick would give them something to record.

Such rage, such anger, such a craving for blood to be exchanged for blood, Nick had broke his right wrist to slip free of his binds. He rose up, knocked the man with the machete in his hands onto the ground. Then Nick ripped off his hood. Once he could see, Nick grabbed the machete, and he butchered everybody in the room. They were in so many pieces that Nick couldn't chop them down into anything finer without the help of a meat grinder.

American operatives showed up soon after Nick killed them all. The Internet feed was terminated. Then the government took in Nick as a ward of the state, trained him, groomed him to destroy threats against America, and here he was, standing in the fucking King's Suite to "let off some steam" and get back into the swing of things.

Thanks America for using me until my mind is a boiling pot of nightmares and self-loathing. Thank you for granting me this wonderful opportunity to recover from my killing spree by gambling and sleeping in an overpriced glass box. Thanks, Uncle Sam! High five, and fuck you.

No more.

This. Ends. Now.

Goddamn them for taking advantage of me. I've slaughtered hundreds of people. I want to be the person I used to be.

Mom and Dad, I died when you died. You wouldn't be proud of the way I turned out.

How dare they take my life away from me!

Nick was balled up on the floor, weeping, cursing, shouting, and punching the floor to unleash the deep down inner turmoil that plagued his existence. He couldn't stop seeing his horrible past, the butchery, the death, the executions, the torture, and the lakes of blood he'd created in the name of America.

How would he go on with life?

He could kill himself in that fancy hot tub.

Or, maybe he would jump through the glass window, fall some forty-odd stories, and give something for those tourists really to take pictures of.

There was plenty of booze in the room. He could drink, and drink, and drink, until he blacked out, and blacked out for good.

The phone rang.

Nick's raging-hell-called-thoughts abruptly stopped.

He picked up the phone, and did his best to remove the anguish from his voice.

"Hello?"

Nick forgot all about her.

Audra Merrit.

Every horror beyond imagination vanished when he heard that sweet voice talk on the other end of the line.

Heath Bitterwell

The War Room mimicked a giant security office. Hundreds of screens featured constant feeds of the casino. The gaming floor. The slot machines. The room of ice sculptures that looked like movie stars. The buffets. The giant "Wheel of Cash" that spun every other hour for a random patron to win big. The moneybox, a tall glass cage that shot dollar bills from the floor for sixty seconds, while some idiot inside did their best to grab what they could in sixty seconds. Heath had a view of every angle of the gaming floor.

Nobody could outdo The Bitterwell Casino. Heath had hundreds of more slot machines than any other casino in Vegas. Heath also had them beat with the number of card tables. His gaming rooms were lavish and insane. Free drinks weren't enough on the gaming floor. The patrons wanted variety, class, and to win, win, win. If the competition tried to outdo him, he'd clear more space, add more machines, more card tables, and continue his domination on the Vegas market.

However, this visit to the War Room wasn't about the gaming floor.

This was about Nick Folder.

Sid worked the control panel. The panel was connected to a giant computer that gave them video access to specific rooms, floors, and even identifies previously identified cheaters returning to the gambling floor by means of facial identification. There was a lot more that the control panel could do, but for now, Heath thought, keeping on top of Nick Folder was the main priority.

When they queued up the security feed in the King's Suite, what they saw had them both reeling in shock. Nick was sprawled out on the floor. The man's head was thrown back, releasing horrible sounds of anguish. The man was throwing an emotional fit.

Sid was puzzled. "Is he having a heart attack?"

"No," Heath said, "I think he's having a nervous breakdown."

"Then he's a threat to nobody, sir. That's excellent."

Heath wasn't so sure. "The guy's clearly unhinged. Did you see him before he got his makeover? He looked as if he had crawled out of hell's asshole. I still don't know his angle. Why would I get that message saying to treat Nick like a God from the Secretary of Defense? I don't feel any better about the matter. In fact, I feel worse to know he's got a kink in his slinky."

"Let me kill him," Sid insisted. "I'll lure him out of the casino. I'll get him downtown, around Freemont Street, or maybe at one of those other crackerjack hotels and strip joints. I'll make it look like he bought a cheap hooker, and he overdosed on heroin in his bed. I got the shit to do it. If he's so upset, nobody would question an unsound man's reason for offing himself. We need to get him out of your casino as soon as possible."

Heath noted the words on the screen monitoring Nick's room. It said he was getting a call from the sixth floor from a woman named Audra Merrit.

Audra was the key, Heath thought.

"This is why Nick's here," Heath said. "That woman. What do we know about her?"

Sid was on the security panel, accessing the casino's guest database. "I see she's from Iowa. She came a long way to see this asshole. It could be two people just hooking up. Audra might not have a thing to do with Nick's other motives for being here. She's just a piece of ass."

"We can still use her if we need to."

Heath lit up a cigar. He would really like a roll in the sack with one of his cocktail girls right about now. His fetish was drinking shots out of their navels, then making it burn when he went down on the girls. The sounds they made. A shock. A whinny. The burn on their clits. *Oh*, how it thrilled him to do it.

"I want to wait," Heath decided. "We might have to let things play out first. Maybe I'm being paranoid. It could be nothing."

"You're being a careful businessman," Sid said. "If you'll allow me, sir, I can keep tabs on Nick and this woman. I'll follow their every moments. If you want to stay up here while I go about my normal duties, and tell me what's up, we can contain the situation, if it's a situation."

"What would I do without you, Sid? Stay on them. I'll tell you what to do from up here."

"Yes, sir."

Sid was about to leave the war room when Heath said, "Oh, and Sid."

"Yes, sir."

"Send in a few of my cocktail girls."

Chopper Dan

"Blow him a new asshole. Rearrange that ugly face. Fuck him up, boys. Turn him into a steaming pile of fuck. Squash him! Bury him under a heap of shit! BASH SOME ASS!"

Chopper Dan was cheering the naval fleet on, even though his radio didn't work, and nobody could hear him. He had to do something, because his nerves had him on edge. He could only watch the battle go down from his aerial position.

B2 Bombers and dozens of other assault aircrafts launched missiles at the giant beast.

Soooooooooooooooooooooooooonk!

Soooooooooooooooooooooooooonk!

Soooooooooooooooooooooooooonk!

Navy vessels were blasting machine guns and following up the reports with more missile attacks. Everywhere, the booms and crashes of war resounded.

Chopper Dan anticipated the beast to blow up into flying chunks of dog food. Its guts would slap the helicopter. He would have to buy new wiper blades because the mess would be so thick. Its body parts would become steaming buoys on the water. The horror would be over, and this would be fodder for the news. Scientific teams would create new studies and write textbooks on this anomaly's existence.

None of that would happen, because the monster wasn't going down so easily.

The monster's eyes throbbed in it sockets. Those enormous globular eyes turned completely ultraviolet red, the red overtaking the black. It threw back its head, and shrieked:

Raaaaaaaaaaaaaaaaaaaaaaaatch!

Right before the first rocket reached striking distance, the beast tensed its arms, tightened its body, and suddenly, a neon green aura of light surrounded the beast. Every missile was absorbed by that overwhelming light. The missiles simply disintegrated. No booms. No explosions. Just gone.

The green aura vanished.

Dan watched the beast's plated body grow in strength. New bulging muscles formed along its back. The bones jutting out of its back extended even longer. The beast was turning into something even more powerful and destructive.

Dan braced himself for the worst.

The monster's red bulbous orb eyes were hideous and angry as it leveled destruction upon the open water.

The reptile's mouth doubled in size, and out rolled a black tongue that kept extending and extending. The tongue cracked like a whip, slashing a navy aircraft carrier into pieces. Out from under its tongue, something sprayed a golden fountain of fizzing rain. The rain struck the assault aircrafts. The substance melted steel, and in seconds, caused the aircrafts to erode and explode. The pilots who had hit the eject button suffered the worst. As the pilots were falling from the sky after deploying their parachutes, the acid was eating into their bodies and turning them into screaming, melting, half-skeletal victims.

The monster reached back and pulled out one of the spines from its back. It launched the jagged bone at another aircraft carrier. When it hit, it was a green ooze bomb. The steel structure was see-through in seconds. The naval officers inside were turned inside out, then melted down to nothing. The hideous demon smashed the dozen other aircraft carriers with its powerful fists. The violent game of whack-o-mole cost hundreds of lives.

The beast wasn't done yet. It dove down into the ocean. Chopper Dan could see brilliant bursts of yellow and orange light explode every few seconds. Whatever submarine attack the United States had planned, the monster ended the retaliation.

The beast didn't come back up to surface.

Chopper Dan could see those twin red eyes glow beneath the surface. It was swimming onwards. Where to, he didn't know.

"Oh, I don't think so, you ugly son-of-a-bitch. You're not getting away, fuck meat."

Chopper Dan kept tracking the beast. The monster simply ravaged anything in its way. It had unique killing abilities. He still couldn't believe what he'd just witnessed.

Chopper Dan named it Ravager.

He was determined to be the one who killed this thing. Thousands of lives were clearly at risk. The ocean was deathly silent now. The scattered remains of aircraft carriers and submarines floated on the water, still smoldering and being dissolved by the monster's spit/saliva combo, or whatever poison had sprayed from its poisonous mouth.

Chopper Dan hovered above the monster. He prayed he didn't go down like the rest of those ships. He had no defense, or means of retaliation.

I will kill you.

Ravager, be damned.

Sentiments were shit, Chopper Dan reasoned. Ravager was headed straight for the United States. It wouldn't be much longer before it swam to California.

Where are you really headed?

What's drawing you to the coast?

If he could make contact with somebody, he could ask someone to do some quick research about what the Ravager could really be. If such research existed.

The radio still didn't work.

Useless! I only have one other option.

Chopper Dan tried his cell phone.

"Fuck yeah! I got a signal. You're screwed, Ravager. I'll see you dead, you big piece of shit."

He dialed Kathy Ingrid's number, and prayed his old friend answered the call.

Nick Folder

There was something about Audra Merrit's voice over the phone that rescued Nick from his personal hell. She expected good things of Nick, because she only remembered good things about him from their younger years. Nick reconnected with her online through a dating page just months ago. It was what lonely soldiers and government goons did between jobs, especially when they were looking for that piece of humanity that used to be inside them before killing became a normal way of life.

Audra and Nick were friends in high school. They went on one date together, before Audra attended Iowa State University and moved on with her life. They lost touch, or more accurately, Nick dropped off the face of the earth after his terrible trip to Afghanistan and the execution of his parents. Audra did what any normal person did when someone didn't return their calls. They moved on.

There was a knock at Nick's suite door.

Nick was suddenly nervous. After Audra had called his room, he rushed to dry his eyes, threw back a quick shot of bourbon, and composed himself.

So much time had passed since he had last seen Audra. They were so young and untried by life back then. He could only imagine how this reunion would go.

Nick double-checked his face.

He appeared to be halfway normal.

Just try to have some fun. She came all this way. You owe her that much.

Nick steeled himself by taking in a deep breath. He opened the door, and there she was, Audra Merrit, in the flesh. You could've torn her picture out of their senior yearbook, and she would look nearly the same. The only thing that had changed, she had dyed her hair black when she used to be dirty blonde. She had tattoos going down both arms. Audra had done some living since the last time Nick had seen her. Twice divorced. One estranged daughter. Some drug use. Definite alcohol abuse. Audra had the cleaned up look of someone trying hard to start over. What she'd done, who'd broken her heart, and her regrets and mistakes mattered nothing to Nick. The only thing that mattered to Nick was that she knew him as the Nick Folder he once was, and that was good enough.

Audra's green eyes lit up. She shut the door behind her and locked it. She didn't comment about the over-the-top accommodations in the room.

"You're not married, and you're not dating anyone?"

"No."

"Kids?"

"No kids."

Audra lifted off her shirt, unbuttoned her bra, and showed him her breasts. Each nipple had two steel hoops through them.

"I'm going to skip right to it, Mr. Nick. You wanna fuck me in that hot tub?"

She hiked down her skirt, and she sashayed out of her panties.

Nick felt a heat burn in his core.

"Yes I do."

Nick realized he was wearing too many clothes. He stripped down to nothing and joined his old friend in the hot tub.

Thank God for you, Audra Merrit.

Ray Desanti

Ray was done waiting. Now was the time to engage. He checked his watch. Five-thirty on the dot. Ray drove up the street and parked his van near The Luxor. He reported into the walkie, "Blast-o-van prepared."

He left the van parked on the street. Ray walked by the neighboring casinos, trying to stay inconspicuous. Signs everywhere promoted hot slots, cheap steak dinners, buffets, and strong cases to empty your wallets into the city.

Ray would give them a real jackpot.

He checked his watch again. Thirty seconds until the blast-o-van did its job. That gave him more time to put distance between him and the vehicle before the diversion began.

Ray called the ten other vans parked along the same block as The Bitterwell Casino, including the six surrounding The Bitterwell Casino itself. This would cause riots. It would also buy them time to infiltrate the casino, slip through security, and really put Heath's operation in a full nelson.

Ray called each checkpoint.

Everybody was on the ball.

He had one helluva team. Big time money gave a bunch of criminals serious incentive to get their shit together. When thieves get a whiff of billions of dollars, it was enough to turn dipshits into Rhode Scholars.

Ray had no idea what he would have to do to escape The Bitterwell Casino tonight alive. Money and revenge would be the last things on his mind by the time the night was through.

Five seconds remaining until the vans did their job.

Ray thought back to how it was a miracle he survived those four gunshots to the belly, and who administered them. The cartel goons were enjoying themselves at The Bitterwell Casino. They better eat the finest steaks and drink up the finest, most expensive spirits, he thought. Tonight would be their final farewell. Ray would see to it. He had learned many modes of self-defense. Karate. Tai-kwon-do. Black Medicine. Ray had read up on pressure points, and how to prolong one's death.

Tonight, Ray would become a death dragon.

Ray turned to in time to witness his van at work. The driver's side and passenger side doors opened by the automatic system he installed. From the vehicle's speakers, an automated voice boomed: "PAYBACK'S A BITCH! PAYBACK'S A BITCH! PAYBACK'S A BITCH!"

The crowds on the sidewalks, and those standing inside nearby casinos overheard the commotion. Fear and confusion spread.

The tourist's were going to get it real good, Ray thought.

...*five, four, three, two, ONE!*

POP! POP! POP! POP!

Streams of confetti blasted out of the van's doors, followed up by dollar bills shooting out onto the streets for half a block in each direction. People stampeded the area, fighting and shoving against each other, as money rained down upon them.

The gamble was an expensive rouse.

Ray prayed it worked.

He was running against the tide of people hurrying to get a piece of the green action. When he arrived at the back loading dock area of The Bitterwell Casino, the security officers were nowhere to be seen. Nobody else was in a good distance of them either.

No witnesses, Ray thought, *no problem.*

Money was flying everywhere, and nobody wanted to miss out on a single buck. Even the dumbass security guards were into it. Nobody could resist a scene when something so cool was happening.

Ray stood back from the main security gate that led into the back loading dock of The Bitterwell Casino. He commanded into his walkie, "Okay to go! Smash through!"

A semi-truck rolled around the corner. Picking up speed, the front became a battering ram that sent the black steel gate flying off its hinges. Ray ran after the semi. Once they reached the docking area, the dangerous work would begin.

Chopper Dan

Pick up.

For God's sake, this is important.

Can you blame her for not answering your call? Kathy Ingrid probably thinks you're the biggest asshole in the world. Maybe I am, but this is too important to let petty bullshit get in the way of saving lives.

Damn it, pick up!

I need you, Kathy.

The relationship between Kathy and Dan was the very definition of having a bridge burned. Chopper Dan reported the morning weather from his whirly bird, while Kathy Ingrid stayed back at the News Channel five studio reporting the general news, and would talk to Dan via "Skyview" camera to deliver the morning traffic rundown.

Chopper Dan had worked for nineteen years at News Channel Five. The problem, after his painful divorce, and his wife quickly remarrying and relocating to Paris with the kids, Dan started taking to drinking. One morning on the job, he was flying the chopper drunk. Dan didn't realize he had his headset microphone on, and every word he said to himself filtered over Kathy reporting how a local kindergarten kid saved a flock of geese from a BB gun totting group of bullies.

"Can't win shit in this world. You treat a girl right, you're a breadwinning son-of-a-gun, and the bitch still has to be a real vagina about the situation. I mean moving and taking the kids to Paris, of all places! You might as well shove my kids up Antarctica's asshole! I won't get to see them ever. She did it on purpose. Paris? I mean, seriously. Parlez-vous, français? More like parlez-vous, fuck you!

"And you know what else is bad? I haven't been laid in six months. That's a drought. No life can be sustained in this dried up desert called my cock. Even the vultures have moved on to greener pussy pastures. I'm Chopper Dan. Why can't I get laid? Are the women in Seattle that uptight? Shove a pencil up there, and it'd get sharpened down to the eraser.

"Can't win, can't win, can't win, but man, oh man, talk about Kathy Ingrid. What a sweet peach! I hear she doesn't wear panties underneath that news desk. It's a nerves thing. You let that thing air out, and you can read words off the teleprompter like a Goddamn thespian. I'd give her a cure to those nerves. The cure? My dick! Blast off, baby!

"I shouldn't say those things. I'm just drunk. Really drunk. Kathy's great. I love her. I need to take a piss. Maybe if I take it out the side door, nobody will notice piss raining down on the interstate. I mean, it's Seattle! The city's a latrine. A feces freeway.

"Wait...is this thing on? Uh-oh."

Chopper Dan was fired after the incident. He issued a public apology, attended "AA" meetings, and served six months jail for flying drunk. No mattered how many times he tried to apologize to Kathy in person, she refused to hear it. He accomplished many things in his personal life to better himself, including his numerous visits to Paris, much to the chagrin of his ex-wife, to see his children.

He never imagined being in this current situation, chasing some kind of mega-lizard across the ocean. This was his chance to do good in the world again.

Chopper Dan wouldn't be that asshole who said those terrible things on the air.

He would be a hero.

If only Kathy Ingrid would answer his call.

Pick.

The.

Fuck.

Up.

Kathy.

He thought it was going to go to voicemail, when a hesitant voice answered. "Dan, is that really you? Boy, you got some nerve."

Was she going to hang up on him? He couldn't tell if her voice rang with curiosity or anger, so he started talking, and he made it fast.

"I know I'm a piece-of-shit. No apology will ever make it up to you, but people's lives are in danger. This isn't about me and you, I promise."

"Is this some kind of trick your immature brain drummed up to get me to talk to you? And for your information, I've never once done a news report without underwear on, you stupid jerk."

"Wait, I'm sorry, I'm *sooooooo* sorry. You have to listen to me now, or lots of people are going to die! Please, Kathy. I'm begging you to help me."

"Why should I help you? And are you flying? They should've banned you from the sky for life, for what you did. Flying over Seattle drunk. You're nothing more than a lush with a teenager's brain. Men never change. Dick for brains. Dick for everything!"

"I could be dead at any moment, Kathy. This is the most important thing I could do with my life. I thought of you, because you're a reporter. You're great with research and drumming up the truth. You're reliable."

"You're a loser," Kathy growled. "How dare you call me? Did you know people at the office still look at me as if I'm some kind of slut? It's all of your fault, Dan. Oh, I'm sorry, let me call you by your real name. Chopper Dan. More like *Chopper Asshole*."

He really had to put it on the line. He didn't know anybody else with the right credentials that could help him identify this beast and kill it.

"I was wrong and I had no right. I know nothing will ever change or make better of what I did. If you don't want to help me, maybe you'll be willing to help the United States Navy?"

Kathy paused.

She was interested, and Dan knew it.

"Go on."

Chopper Dan explained the job he was doing on Chichi-Hama Island, and about the beast that rose up from the ground. He knew as he was talking that the details were unbelievable, and Kathy might dismiss him outright.

He still had to try.

"Please, if you can look up anything that would indicate that a big monster could possibly come up out of the ground on that island, you have to tell me. You have to contact somebody else to help the Navy. Warn the coast. This thing's coming, and it'll smash and kill everything in sight. Kathy, if you would--"

Kathy had hung up.

Chopper Dan wasn't sure who else to contact. He could've ran down a list of names of other people to help him.

The time for that had expired.

Ravager's two giant globular eyes rose up from the water's surface. Chopper Dan hovered in place. He didn't advance, nor did he retreat.

What did the monster plan to do?

Those eyes trembled in their sockets. They bulged, shrank, bulged, shrank. The eyes were completely red earlier, and now they were mostly black with little red circles in the middle again. The eyes were like mood rings.

What's on your mind, dick wad?

You going to pitch another fit?

Chopper Dan wished he had machine guns or missiles on his chopper. He would reduce this monster to toothpaste.

He remembered the green aura around the beast, and how it had absorbed the missiles and turned that energy into its own killing fuel.

Back at the island, only one thing seemed to deliver Ravager pain. He had to get back to land and get supplies. He had to warn the right persons about what he knew. Chopper Dan didn't have any military contacts. He wanted to dial the police, but his phone wasn't getting a signal anymore.

Chopper Dan prayed that Kathy would look into the matter.

Another problem fighting this thing, his chopper was running low on fuel. He probably didn't have enough to make it back to land. He had used up so much fuel hovering in place.

I guess I won't be a hero, after all.

No redemption for Chopper Dan. My life might as well be flushed down the toilet. My accomplishments mean nothing up against my drunken ramblings on live television.

Ravager's eyes were suddenly giant red globes again.

Chopper Dan froze in terror.

The beast leaped from the ocean, going airborne. The giant claw hand seized the helicopter in its clutches, and pitched the chopper across the ocean.

Nick Folder

"You knew we were going to have sex," Audra teased Nick. "Keep saying you didn't see it coming. Lie to me. I'm okay with that. I just like to cut through the bullshit. It's not like you put up much of a fight."

Nick had his arm around Audra. They were both naked in the hot tub after enjoying a wild romp. Their sex was hungry, grasping, biting, hard pumping, and for Nick, the best release he had in years.

They looked on through the window at the rest of Vegas and talked about their crazy situation.

"I didn't know what to expect," Nick said, honestly. "I only wanted to catch up with an old friend, and I don't know about you, but when a woman as attractive as you gets into her birthday suit, I can't help myself. When I saw the piercings you had down there, then I *really* couldn't help myself. It's your fault this happened."

Audra threw her head back and laughed. "Oh please, I know men. You're single, I'm single, and we're both unattached. You think back to the good ol' days of being young, and you think, 'Man, I really wish I tapped her.' That's what you were thinking. I mean, I reached out to you online, and you were all over me. You wanted me in the sack. If I didn't make the first move, you would've."

"Sure."

"*Sure*? That's all you got to say? *Sure*? You're full of it, Nick. Why else would you agree to meet me in Las Vegas, of all places, so spur of the moment? I'll admit what you won't. It's not a bad thing what we want from each other. After being single for so long, I started to look back at the people I used to date. I searched for people to hook up with, and if that makes me sad, or pathetic, then whatever. Fine. I'm sad. I'm pathetic. There's nothing wrong with knowing what you want, and skipping right to it. I wanted to fuck you. I craved excitement, and here I am, getting it."

Audra wanted Nick to admit he still had the hot's for her all of these years. That part was probably true if he'd had the time and sanity to enjoy the things normal people do in life. She wouldn't understand why he was being so vague about his feelings.

Could she handle an explanation?

"You want me to cut through the bullshit, Audra? I mean, really cut through it?"

"Of course. I just let you explore my body. The least bit you can do is let me explore your mind."

Nick sighed. "This will change the tone of the conversation."

"We're adults, Nick. I don't know what you could tell me that could upset me."

"You remember our only date, and then you went off to college, and I dropped off of the map?"

Audra nodded. "I remember not being able to get in contact with you. Your phone was disconnected. Your friends had no idea what happened to you. Your house was put on the market. Everything I did to try to find you failed. So, I assumed you had moved somewhere, and I wasn't a part of that journey. It happens. When you're that young, people drift apart."

Nick told her about the trip to Afghanistan and the death of his parents, and about how the government had used him as a killing machine against the more potent threats against America.

Audra wore an odd expression on her face that said, 'Is he full of shit, or is he telling me the truth?' She wasn't saying much of anything after Nick told his story. The bubble jets in the hot tub were the only sounds between them.

"You think I'm lying to you?"

Audra stepped out of the tub, dried herself off, and started to put her clothes back on. She had tears in her eyes. That's when Nick knew he made a mistake. She didn't believe him. The story was unbelievable, even if it was the truth.

Sobbing, "You could've said we lost touch after our date, and left it at that. I wouldn't have pressed you for explanations. I've gone on plenty of one-time dates in my life. I can't count the number of times I've arranged dates online, and the person was either a total jerk, or they didn't show up. It hurts me to think you needed to lie to me like that, Nick.

"I remember you being a good guy. You treated women like women wanted to be treated. I was jealous of the girls you dated in high school. I wanted to be that girl holding hands with you in the hallway. This bullshit story...I don't know what you intended for me to think."

Nick stood out of the tub. Water was dripping down his body and pooling on the floor. He was getting cold, standing there. Nick didn't care. She had to understand why he told her the truth.

"I've never been able to talk to anyone about my real life, Audra. The government forced me to keep the secret. This is the first time they let me loose for longer than twenty-four hours to relax."

Nick pointed out the dozens of scars on his body. His back was covered in whip lashing marks. Nick had been cut open and shown his own guts when a rogue group of Islamic extremists wanted Nick to tell them the truth about the mission he was on when captured. He was missing three of his toes on one foot when he stepped on a landmine. Lucky for Nick, the landmine was sort of a dud, and it only used a tiny fraction of its blasting potential. Audra was eyeballing him like he was lunatic as he catalogued his scars and told the stories behind them.

"Why can't men be honest? Just tell me you wanted to fuck me, and leave it that? I don't know how you got those scars on your body, Nick. There's something wrong with you. Hell, I think there's something wrong with me for liking you after all of these years."

She was about to storm out of the King's Suite.

"Listen," Nick said, "I'm telling you the truth. I swear it. I was only trying to be directly honest, because you were honest with me. I jumped the gun. This isn't fun stuff to talk about. I just wanted to open my heart to you, and my timing was awful. I'm going to get dressed, and then I'm going down to that steak restaurant. Join me if you want to start over. If you don't show up, I'll leave you alone, but please understand, I'm being honest. I swear to you."

Audra's face was full of insecurity.

Nick decided it was time to leave her to her thoughts. He had said too much too soon. The mistake would cost him. He left his room, and then he headed down to the steak restaurant wondering if Audra would meet him for dinner, or leave his life for good.

Heath Bitterwell

Heath enjoyed watching Nick and Audra screw. They went at it like two teenagers. Heath had paid women to make love to each other in front of him, and he'd watched plenty of adult movies in his day, but there was nothing like watching two people actually into each other fuck to their heart's content.

Another nice thing, he was watching it all go down while his cocktail girls massaged him and made comments about how they wished Heath would throw them around in bed. He couldn't focus on that now. Nick and Audra were arguing in heated fashion.

This was perfect, Heath thought, when Nick left the suite. He followed Nick's movements to the elevator, and down to the first floor, into Ribald's Wood Fired Steaks.

Audra was alone. She stood there sobbing, talking to herself, and trying to reason through what Nick had told her.

Heath had to know what Nick said to her. Maybe Audra knew the reason for Nick being here. He only had a small window of time to learn what Audra knew without Nick's interference. Heath contacted Sid and told the head of security to meet him at Nick's suite.

Six of the topless women smiled at Heath.

"You're not working again, are you, Heathy baby?"

"Why don't you keep us warm?"

"I want to play. Don't you want to play with me, Heathy?"

"We can share you, Heathy baby."

"Please don't go."

"Later," Heath said, "this is business. Pleasure suffers when business suffers. Don't worry. Once I get this worked out, I'm doing coke off of your sweet asses and riding you to fucking glory, but for now, I got important work to do."

The cocktail girls knew what that meant. They scurried out of the war room like little bunnies and returned to their waiting room. They would return when Heath was good and ready to eye some hot babe flesh. Right now, the way Heath was feeling, the only way he wanted to see skin was in bleeding form.

Heath left the locked up part of the corridor and headed to Nick's room.

Audra had some questions to answer, and Heath knew just how to make her answer them.

Ray Desanti

The back of the semi-truck shot open. Out poured two dozen of Ray's workers. Those who parked the other blast-o-vans met up with Ray in the coming minutes. Now was the time to move. There was no talk, only hand signals. Thirty men and women comprised the team. Each were dressed in black outfits, Kevlar bullet-proof vests, headsets, and heavily armed with a varied collections of arms: riot guns, tear gas launchers, Mossberg, Carbine, Remington, and Winchester shotguns, M-16's, Uzis, Mac-10's, Walter PPK's, AK-47's, Gatling guns, flame throwers, and grenade launchers. Any civilian who saw them coming would jump out of their skins, and run the other way.

Ray's blood was pumping hard as they approached the back door. It was locked, and they knew it would be locked. Ray motioned for Clutch to strap the brick of C-4 against the door.

"Ten seconds," Clutch shouted, moving everybody back. "The explosion isn't huge, but it's got enough kick, it'll blow your balls out the back of your head if you're too close. Get back!"

After the countdown, the C-4 did its job, and then some. It blew up the door, and half the wall. Everything in the general area went up into burning tatters of wood and shards of brick.

A small team of security officers from inside the casino opened fire. Ray's team spent four-hundred rounds in fifteen seconds. The seven security members inside were sent packing to hell in chewed up cabbage form.

"Move it," Ray shouted, "do your job. Careful not to shoot innocent people."

Ray entered the back area that was a stock room of food, booze, and a fully functioning kitchen. They opened fire on the stock, blowing up boxes and destroying expensive goods.

The plan was simple. Shoot up the place and search every floor until they found Heath and made the son-of-a-bitch give up his riches. In the meantime, they would execute the cartel members staying in the casino. Number one priority was robbing the place, and putting a serious dent in the drug cartel's economy.

Ray shot at the ceiling when they came across the kitchen workers. "Stay on the ground. Don't move. Don't go anywhere, and nothing will happen to you. Don't do as I say, and you can take a look at your buddies in the back chocked full of holes. I am not fucking around."

The team secured the kitchen area. They were headed out to the lobby, where things would get complicated. Innocent people were checking into their rooms, while other tourists were gambling out on the gaming floor.

Ray chose the best people for the job. They would stay on point, and do their best not to harm innocent people. Ray had no idea what he'd gotten into, and neither did his team.

Once they exited the kitchen and raised hell in the lobby, nothing would play out the way they expected.

Chopper Dan

Waves of flames spread across the ocean's surface. Whatever fuel he had remaining in the chopper was burning fast. Chopper Dan couldn't connect the dots between the monster throwing the helicopter across the ocean, and him waking up and thrashing in the water for his life. He clutched onto a piece of floating steel that used to be the underbelly of his transport. The rest of the chopper was scattered wreckage that was twisted up, gnarled, and smashed. The beast had literally taken the chopper and cast it across the water as if it was skipping rocks.

Chopper Dan did his best to make sense of the present moment. Blood was running down the side of his face. The red was filling up his right eye. He was dizzy, confused, weak, and unable to do much of anything except hang onto that piece of metal and pray he didn't drown.

Waves were hitting him hard. The ocean was struck by an unnatural tide. Ravager kept smashing his balled up fists against the water. Those red eyes bulged hideous and raving mad. The bone spines along its back extended further out. The beast was getting good and pissed off. Every muscle in its body bulged with power. Ripples of strength spread across its plated body.

A larger air attack was taking place in the sky. Military helicopters, assault jets, and more aircraft carriers loomed on the horizon. Ravager was ready to take them all on. Before it could spit acid, create its protective green aura, or dive into the ocean, a heat-seeking missile pounded the Ravager's back. Two of its bone spines shattered. Ravager was shoved hard into the water. The beast released a shriek of angry surprise.

Two more missiles pounded into its back. Wild claps of thunder rocked the ocean. Shards of its black plated back landed across the water. When the Ravager slammed body-first into the ocean, the concussion caused a massive wave to strike Chopper Dan. Forced off of his only hold, he tried to swim and keep himself above the water. That was the moment he realized how busted up he was from the wreck. A broken arm, he thought, several broken ribs, and his left leg felt like bones were broken on the inside. The agony would've driven him to give up and drown, if it weren't for what he saw next. The Ravager remained under the water. There was no telling what lasting damage those sneaky missiles had inflicted.

The Ravager, Chopper Dan's injuries, they all vanished when he saw what floated on the ocean's surface. The shattered pieces of the Ravager's back seemed to dissolve in the water. The black fizzed into a bright red. Then the pieces exploded.

Something within was breaking out.

Chopper Dan blinked more blood out of his eyes. He reached for what used to be the driver's seat to his helicopter and hung on. Not that it would do him any good.

Death was coming.

They appeared in menacing droves. Each was red, black, yellow, and dark green in color. Chopper Dan imagined the body of carpenter ants, giant praying mantis eyes, the heads of rhinoceros beetles, complete with an extended serrated horn jutting out of its head, and razor sharp mandibles to chew you up. Their legs weren't stick-like, but instead covered in powerful muscle tissue and a complex system of veins. Sixteen legs apiece, the hybrid insect creatures were paddling towards Chopper Dan in a collective front. He imagined them to be bugs, parasites, or some kind of prehistoric mite that had lived under the Ravager's plates.

Man, I'm fucked.

Kiss my ass goodbye. I'm bug food.

The way he was feeling, he welcomed death. Chopper Dan felt so depleted. He kept imagining the way Kathy Ingrid despised him. His ex-wife loathed him. The only people who loved him were his children. They considered him a hero. Any child would if they had a dad who could fly them over the city in an awesome helicopter. Maybe he hadn't completely fucked up, if he could successfully bring life into this world.

My kids love me. Fuck my ex-wife. Fuck the public, and most of all, fuck these monsters.

Chopper Dan reached for the orange floating box within easy arm's reach. He opened it with one hand, and aimed the flare gun right at the crimson ant-faced, beetle-horned, ant-bodied mutant bug that was about to latch onto him.

"Eat some heat!"

The bug was close enough and Chopper Dan fired the flare directly into its mouth. The red head turned an ultraviolet purple before going up into flames. Green bug brains blasted out its eyes and the back of its head in steamy chunks.

One shot fired, and he already had to reload.

This battle was going to be short, he thought, as dozens more of the bugs were coming his way. The way they trashed at the water collectively, he could only see cross-sections of feelers, clicking mandibles, and muscular legs trash and kick up waves.

Chopper Dan tried to reload the flare gun. He only had one more shot. Before he could fire it into the crowd, up from the water, Ravager resurfaced. The green aura surrounded its body. It flew up into the sky as if spring-ejected from the ocean floor. Its arms and legs were sticking straight down as if it was mimicking a rocket. Green glowing vapor trails filled the sky, propelling the monster forward at an incredible flying speed.

How did the monster accomplish such feats?

Back at that island, they had woken a sleeping monster. Nobody could've seen it coming. It could've happened to anybody by mistake. That didn't change the problem. He had to find a way to kill it.

Impossible, he kept thinking. *You're dead. You'll be scattered across the ocean just like your chopper, buddy.*

The fleet of military vehicles was pursuing Ravager.

Chopper Dan was abandoned.

He aimed the flare gun at the swimming horde of creatures.

Well, if I'm dying, there won't be any bullets left in the chamber when I go!

He fired the last flare.

Bugs, be damned.

Nick Folder

Nick knew holding back his emotions was impossible. The last person alive in this world who could consider him a real person had rejected him. He had sprung the truth on Audra too soon. He should've stuck to his story about being an insurance salesman who lived a happy life, with a happy paycheck, and a happy future.

Don't make a scene.

Just drink your drink, sit here, relax a moment, and get it together.

Nick was sitting inside Ribald's Wood-Fired Steaks. He was on the first floor of the casino, sitting at the bar set-up of the restaurant. Nick threw back a stiff shot of bourbon, and immediately asked for another one.

The bartender was in his late fifties. He was dressed in a black suit and tie. He had the esteem of someone who could do better in life, but chose not to for whatever reason.

"Bad day, huh?"

Nick cleared the emotions from his throat. "Yeah, you could say that."

"You clean out your savings in the gaming room?"

"No."

"Well, hey, then you're okay. Money's one thing you can't live without. I don't care what people say about happiness."

"You're awful chatty, aren't you?"

"You look like a guy who needs a man-to-man talk. None of this customer service bullshit. Am I right?"

"Yeah, whatever."

"If there's a problem, it's either women or money. Since you got money, and you're all the better for it, it's gotta be a female problem."

Nick's head was hammering with a migraine. He felt the need to break down and sob and unleash the anguish built up over so many years. His eyes could spring out of their sockets, and what would spill out of his head would be a substance blacker than death, and hotter than hell.

He tried not to look around the room too much.

Nick was starting to see death.

The couple next to him at the bar was waiting for their table. The lady was drinking a martini. The olive was an eyeball. The man was drinking bourbon on the rocks. The rocks were also eyeballs. When the man took a drink, a tiny mouse with the leftovers of a chewed up eyeball took a nose-dive off the rim of the glass.

Jesus, it's happening again.

Those sitting at tables were being served steaks stuck on a long metal stick. It wasn't sizzling steaks Nick was seeing on those sticks. It wasn't beef the blood-faced patrons were mowing down on.

Not here. Not now.

I can't keep doing this.

Nick massaged his forehead. He hammered back the drink. He might as well have been drinking water. It did nothing to put out the fires raging inside of him.

Every bottle of hard liquor on the shelves behind the bartender was packed with bubbling pureed guts.

"Once you lose money, it's impossible to get it back," the bartender said, "but women, if they stray, they might just come back. It's Vegas, baby. Anything's possible here. There's a certain kind of magic in the strip."

"There's also a bunch of shit," Nick said through gritted teeth, "and the magic is an illusion."

"Wow, buddy," the bartender said, "have a drink on me. Top shelf stuff. On the house. The house might always win out there on the gaming floor, but in here, with me, Herb, as your bartender, you might come out on top. I'm going to see you in a better way, fella."

Nick felt the urge to vomit. That would make him feel better. He could purge his life, his past, every dark moment, and somehow, he'd end up with a blank slate. Nick could leave the casino, Vegas, and know nothing of himself.

Could a surgeon do that for him? Just cut it the fuck out?

He didn't want to be a drooling vegetable.

Nick only wanted a new life, not to be mindless.

I'm not going to get any better sitting here in this restaurant.

Nick slapped a twenty-dollar bill onto the counter. He knew Audra wasn't going to meet him down here. She was long gone, and out of his life.

Nick would go up to his room and figure out things within the privacy of four walls.

He retreated faster out of the restaurant when he saw what nastiness was boiling in that "top shelf" bottle of liquor Herb wanted to serve him.

Out of the restaurant, Nick hurried across the gaming floor. The place was packed with people pumping money into slot machines and huddled over the gaming tables. An older woman won at a quarter slot machine. Coins rained into the tray, and the woman filled up her cup as she cheered and hollered in victory. Nick didn't see coins spill out of the machine. He saw fingers, toes, and teeth.

Get out of here before you really lose your shit.

When Nick stumbled into the elevator with beads of sweat pouring down his face and punched the button for his floor, he just missed Ray Desanti's team enter the gaming floor by minutes.

Nick Folder

The people in the hallways gasped at Nick. Several asked if he needed any help. Nick ignored them. What he needed was privacy. He couldn't control the speed of his thoughts. His sanity was about to go off the rails. Nick was barely able to slide his keycard to unlock the door to the King's Suite. Once he entered, he slammed the door closed, and sucked in several deep gulps of breath.

"Hello, Nick Folder."

Nick blinked the stinging sweat from his eyes. He couldn't anticipate the scene happening in the main room. A tall stranger with a bald head had a gun drawn to Audra's head. Audra had a black eye, a busted lip, and blood was oozing from her nose.

The other man was familiar.

Heath Bitterwell.

Heath was sitting on the chair across from the stranger holding Audra by the arm. Heath was smoking a cigar and wearing a delighted expression on his face.

"Meet my associate, Sid Rigard," Heath said. "We've got a few things to talk about. We wanted to have a chat with your friend, Audra. A private conversation, actually, to determine why you're really here, Nick. We thought she'd be helpful, but she didn't know anything. She's...kind of, innocent. We didn't expect you back so soon, pal. While you're here, let's straighten out a few things. I'm a direct man. I know you're up to something. You're investigating me, aren't you?"

Nick didn't hear a word the man said.

Audra's eyes wouldn't leave Nick. They said help me in a thousand different ways. They also said something else. There was an apology in her eyes. She regarded him with concern, maybe even love. The moment was so jilted that Nick couldn't be accurate about anything.

"Let her go," Nick finally said. "Any problem you have with me, let's settle it between each other. No need to hurt her anymore. She's an old friend from school. That's all. We haven't seen in each other since we graduated. Be reasonable, and I'll return the favor."

"Be reasonable," Heath mimicked Nick's stoic voice. "Yeah, like I can trust you. No, we're keeping Audra right here. I mean, I've already showed her my cards. She knows I'm up to something illegal in this casino. I can't let her go. I can't even let her live."

Sid gave Nick a killer's smile.

The son-of-a-bitch enjoyed his boss's tune.

Heath flicked a cigar ash into a glass ashtray that was in the shape of a spade. "You know, I have a batch of women who tend to my every need. When I want sex, they spread their legs. When I want to talk, they listen, and those bitches pretend I'm the best damn thing ever to happen to them. They put on a show for me, because I'm Heath Bitterwell. I make the impossible, possible.

"This casino has so much power, and I'm the only one who can unleash it. That's why I thought the government left me alone. They know what I can accomplish here. I'm a serious threat. I guess them sending you after me was their way of saying I'm too big for my britches. I don't care what they try to do to me. Nobody can tell me what to do, Nick. Not in this building. Not while I'm in it. Nobody. Here, in this casino, *I am God*."

Nick then understood Heath had an even bigger screw loose than he did. The way Heath's eyes brightened when he talked about the casino's ability was strange, as it was frightening.

Nick kept his words simple.

"Please, let Audra go. I'll go along with anything you say. I promise."

Heath exploded, "*You'll go along with anything I say, because I say!* There are no options here. No bargaining, and you know what, Nick? I could've spared Audra's life a little longer. You see, I told you about my girlies. I call them my cocktail girls. They put their tail against my cock when I tell them to. They'd eat the shit out of my ass if I demanded it, but they do it willingly, because I pay them well.

"But Audra here, I couldn't pay her enough to make her do the things I want. There isn't a sum of money great enough for her to bend to my will. I can force her through other modes of coercion. Fear, pain, torture, it's nothing I'm afraid to explore. Believe me, I know all about getting what I want from people who don't want to give it up.

"The problem, Nick, is the way you're looking at me. You're afraid for Audra, but you're not afraid of me, Nick. You're giving me that look that says you're going to kill me. I can put on a show, try to scare you, try to impress you with my resume of dark deeds, but you, Nick, cannot be impressed. So why bother wasting my time using Audra as collateral? It doesn't work in your case. I have to use other modes to get through to you. Audra is useless to me. Sid, go ahead and do your thing."

Sid nodded. "You got it, boss."

Nick crumbled to the floor on all fours. He cried out in horror. This couldn't be happening, but it was, and the outcome was forever final.

Audra was bleeding from the gaping hole in the back of her head. Sid had fired the bullet from his 9mm.

Audra was the last vestige to be salvaged of his former self.

Now, he was back to the person he'd become.

Nick was pissed.

Sid, approaching him like a henchmen, reached out to grab Nick. He didn't expect Nick to leap up to his feet, grab Sid by the neck and right leg, and launch him across the room like a spear. The flailing man crashed through the glass table in the dining area. Sid's landing was in a bed of glass.

The henchman wasn't getting up anytime soon.

Heath was ripped from his megalomaniac's moment of power. "Nick! Nick, now hold on! Let's talk. Nick. No, Nick! Don't!"

Heath reached into his suit pocket for the gun from his shoulder holster. Nick broke the man's wrist like a twig. Agony boiled in Heath's eyes.

That was only beginning. Nick kicked the man back into the chair by a solid blow to the solar plexus. Nick drove his knee into the man's ribcage and heard the rich crack of bones. Nick's fists rained down, turning Heath's face into a bleeding raw pulp. Blood bubbled out of both his nostrils. When Heath spat out blood, teeth rattled onto the floor. Heath's eyes were about to roll up into his head. Death or unconsciousness, Nick didn't know, nor did he care. Nick kept punching, and punching, and punching the evil bastard, until he thought he'd broken bones in his own fists, and still, he kept bringing on the beating.

"How could you? How could you kill her? She was innocent. Audra did nothing to you, and you killed her!"

Heath was unrecognizable when Nick was finished. Nick was out-of-breath and energy. Heath was sprawled out on the ground. Strange hissing and bubbling noises issued from his nose and mouth.

The door was thrown open. Security officers stormed into the room, each with their handguns drawn. Nick wasn't surprised that back up had arrived to help Heath. What did surprise him was the fact they were holding M-16's and automatic handguns.

The security members carted a bleeding, moaning Heath Bitterwell out of the room. "We need to get you out of here. The casino isn't safe, sir."

The security eyed Nick as if he'd cannibalized their boss.

Another set of security carried Sid out of the room. Three of the team stayed behind when the door shut. The goons kept their guns drawn on Nick.

"Don't move," one of them said to Nick. "You're staying here until what's going downstairs is resolved. You try anything, and we have permission to blow your head off. We've dealt with your kind before. You wouldn't be the first we had to kill."

Nick's eyes fell on Audra. She wouldn't be dead if he they hadn't hooked up online. Audra had plenty of life left to live, and now, there was nothing.

Heath said so himself earlier, that something was going on illegal in the casino. Nick would find out what exactly, expose the truth, and take down the operation at any cost.

If I can't live a normal life, then so be it. If I can't keep people safe who once knew me, then I'll remain a stranger to everyone.

Nick shifted his focus from Audra to the three security officers. He knew what he had to do next.

Ray Desanti

Ray spattered M-16 gunfire into the ceiling. "All bets are off, people! Stay on the floor, and shut the fuck up. This is our casino now. Your place is on the floor. We do our business, you don't get in our way, and you'll come out of here without a single bullet in your body. Otherwise, you people will leave here in a body bag."

Ray expected the patrons to be hysterical, and they were. Everybody was shouting, and carrying on in fear. Ray's team unloaded twelve-hundred rounds. Blackjack tables were reduced to splinters and shreds by bursts of hot lead from twelve different gunners. A roulette wheel was launched off of a table, and knocked three running patrons onto the floor. The giant bar in the center of everything was chocked full of so many holes, every big screen television, bottle of liquor, beer tap, and stool was reduced to pieces. Slot machines were blasted. Hundreds of the steel boxes were knocked down, or thrown across the room. Sparks and coins spilled forth onto the gaming floor. People were fighting over the coins, even at gunpoint.

Jesus Christ. The world we live in.

Only one way to get through to these people.

Ray shot five people in the kneecaps. They flailed and cried, spilling blood and unleashing screams.

That took the mob mentality down a notch.

Silence descended upon the gaming floor. The music from the slot machines sounded louder now that people weren't talking. The machines were almost deafening to Ray.

"I'm being generous with you idiots," Ray said. "I could've blown your heads off. I will, if you don't get on the floor and shut your mouths. This isn't about you, so don't make it about you. Let us do our business."

Ray instructed three of his team to return to the back entrance. They placed bricks of C-4 along each doorway. Fifteen others rushed the main doors, placing more bricks of C-4 along each doorway.

"It's simple," Ray addressed everyone, "if any police try and bust through the door and crash the party, I blow this place the fuck up."

He lifted a young woman who probably had just turned twenty-one off the ground by her ponytail. "You got a cell phone, bitch? Of course you do."

The girl was reduced to sobs.

"Dial the police for me, honey," Ray said. "Go ahead. Do it."

The girl forgot how to use her phone for a few moments, and then she got it together. She dialed the police.

"Very good," Ray said. "Now tell the dispatcher The Bitterwell Casino is being taken over by machine gun thugs. If anybody tries to bust through the doors, or crash the party, we're going up sky high. Hundreds of people will die, and the blood will be on the Vegas PD's hands."

After she told the police the message, Ray gave her a hundred dollar bill. "You did good. Now go to that quarter slot. Once you're done, get back down on the floor. Thank you for your help."

She held the hundred-dollar bill with two fingers, and didn't move.

"Yeah, you're probably right," Ray laughed. "Pocket the money. You won't win jack shit on those slot machines. Keep the money, and get down on the floor, kiddo."

Once she was on the ground, Ray motioned for his crew to move on with the next step of the plan. The crew searched the area for Bitterwell casino workers. Once they were rounded up, the idiots in ugly burgundy outfits, looking like bellboys from the 1950's, Ray tried to find the one person who might be able to tell him something useful. Most of the men had that expression of anger and dumb concern. The clash made them look like babies shitting their pants. There was only one person who appeared collected under the pressure.

Her name was Betsy, and she was sixty some years old.

Ray grabbed her by the arm and guided her away from her fellow co-workers. "Okay, Betsy, I want you to phone whoever runs the security cameras in this place. If we can settle this peacefully, I'm all about that. If they refuse, this gaming floor becomes a bloodbath. I'm talking wholesale slaughter. I got enough bullets to put all of you in your graves a hundred times over."

Betsy wasn't impressed with his tough words. She regarded him as a no-good bully. "Who is it you want to talk to? If you're so reasonable, tell me exactly what you want then."

Ray liked this lady.

He really hoped he didn't have to blast her between the eyes.

"I need to contact Heath Bitterwell."

Betsy sneered at him. "And your message?"

"Tell him Ray Desanti is here to take all of his money and to kill all of his friends."

Betsy's cool and collected expression vanished.

The woman steeled herself before trying a variety of channels on her walkie device. She wasn't getting through to anybody. Ray could see the confusion building on her face.

Betsy scowled. "Nobody's answering. The head of security, the head of surveillance, even the customer service people aren't replying. It's like the line of communication has been cut."

When Betsy said that, the music coming from the speakers went silent. From the intercom, an automated voice spoke, and what it had to say rocked everybody, including Ray, to their very cores.

This job was about to get much more complicated...and bloody.

Chopper Dan

Blasting the final flare into the throng of plated creatures was a joke. The shot blew one of the eight-legged creature's mandible right off its beady-eyed face. Chopper Dan was aghast when a new mandible grew in its place in seconds.

He couldn't swim away to save his life. If he had the ability, he would put back together his broken toy of a helicopter and take to the sky.

Think about your children.

You lived a full life. There's nothing more you can do now.

I guess I get to die knowing what it's like to be eaten to death.

Chopper Dan closed his eyes. He couldn't bare to watch the mean insect-crustacean hybrids approach. It was bad enough hearing their clickers, and the sound of suctioning as they masticated, sucked up the spit, masticated again, and splashed and paddled against the water to reach him.

He was just a scrap of meat to be devoured. The culmination of his life's work, his legacy, would end by being sent through a creature's digestive tract and excreted out into the ocean. It was the kind of life perspective only a dying man could truly understand.

Chopper Dan flipped off the crowd of monsters.

"Chopper Dan's final report: FUCK YOU ALL!"

The second he extended his middle finger, a rain of bullets hammered down upon the carnivorous crustaceans. Bug eyes popped. Ant-shaped heads were squashed, smashed in, obliterated, and erased. Thoraxes were reduced to high-flying pulp. Most of them were simply chewed up by the hot hail of bullets. They all resembled crunched up aluminum cans. The ocean was decorated in every color of pus in the insect bodily fluid color wheel.

Dan reeled at his middle finger, and its power. He was so out-of-sorts, he thought his middle finger had beckoned a higher power to bring down a hail of force to stop the monsters. It didn't take long for Dan to realize he was *very* wrong.

A helicopter from the National Guard hovered overhead. A plastic basket for Dan to crawl into was lowered. He struggled to get inside, but once he buckled in, he was hoisted up to safety. Dan looked down at the ocean. The scattered pieces of twitching plated pieces were sickening. He was grateful to be inside the helicopter.

Medics were overlooking his wounds, and while they did so, one of the medics handed him a headset. The worker shouted over the roar of the propellers, "Somebody wants to talk to you!"

Chopper Dan couldn't believe who was on the line.

Kathy Ingrid.

"Reports are all over the news. There's a war going on out in the ocean. It's almost reaching the coast. The monster is...horrible."

"You mean Ravager has almost reached the coast? Shit. If that monster gets onto land, everybody in its path is dead. This thing will slaughter the United States. You have to evacuate the cities."

"We're preparing, Dan," Kathy said. "I'm sorry I was so shitty to you earlier."

"It's in the past. It's right now we have to worry about. You have to tell them, whoever can stop this thing, its weakness."

Chopper Dan told her the Ravager's weakness.

"Nobody will believe that!"

"Try, damn it! I'm on its tail. Don't you worry, Kathy, I'm going to stop it. You see, I'm badly injured. I'm internally bleeding, my guts are squashed, and I'm slowly dying."

"Dan, no. Don't talk like that. You can be saved. What are you saying? I'll do everything I can to help you."

"No time, no way," Dan sighed, "I'm dying. I know it. A man can tell when his time is short, and my fuse is burning fast. I have a score to settle with that motherfucker. I'll see it dead before I'm sleeping six feet under.

"Please, Kathy, accept my apologies. You're a fine, fine woman, and you deserve nothing less than a charmed life. Somewhere in those drunk ramblings that went on the air, I only meant to say you're the kind of woman no man like me could ever have, but I still wanted you anyway. You can't blame me for my ambitions, pretty lady.

"Now tell the world how to stop this thing. If I fail, I pray somebody else succeeds. Consider it a dying man's wish, Kathy. Stay out of the Ravager's path. Help me put this beast to sleep. If I can't, I don't know who can."

"Dan, no. Wait a second, and hear me out!"

Chopper Dan took off the headphones.

His time was short. He knew his internal injuries would lead him to his death. He could see it in the medics' face. Chopper Dan was a dead man.

A dead man with nothing to lose.

Chopper Dan talked to the pilot. "You boys up for killing this tall son-of-a-bitch?"

The crew of three wasn't sure what to say.

"This thing's got guns and rockets, right? That's about all I need."

Chopper Dan reached towards the nearest medic and grabbed his Desert Eagle pistol from his holster. "Okay, I'm commandeering this whirly bird. This is a one-way ride, and you boys aren't ready to punch in your ticket. I fucking am. Now take a dive into the ocean. I mean it. You know I'm a dead man, and I've got nothing to lose."

The medics tried to talk him down.

Chopper Dan shot one in the foot.

"Take the plunge, asshole!"

That did the trick.

The bleeding foot guy was the first to take a finely executed dive. His partner was next. He did an awkward sideways flail down into the ocean.

That left the pilot.

"Put it on automatic, good sir," Dan said, staying in the back so the pilot could maneuver out the side. "Sorry to do this to you. I know what a man's helicopter means to him. It's nothing personal. I'm not trying to step on your dick."

Chopper Dan couldn't see the pilot's face through his helmet, the way the sun hit the plastic, but he could tell the man was sincere just by his words.

"As I see it, you know the most about this thing, Dan. I've seen that beast in action. It's all over the news. Someone has to step up and get the job done. This is your last mission. You can't fail. All I can tell you is that this bird is fully fueled. It was last reported the monster was cutting through California and pointed right for Nevada. God help them. You must save those people. If you know how to stop it, then stop it."

The California coast was visible up ahead.

"I won't let you down," Chopper Dan said. "Now get the fuck off of my helicopter!"

Nick Folder

Heath Bitterwell wasn't dead. His henchman, Sid, if he recalled the fucker's name, was helped out of the room. Sid was barely conscious on the way out. Heath and Sid both had their hands in Audra's death. Her final moments in this world were full of terror. Nick could never reconcile that fact. What Nick could reconcile, was a heavy dose of revenge.

Audra's corpse remained on the floor.

Nick asked one of the security goons in the room, "What will you do with her body?"

The three security guards standing in front of the door were startled by Nick's deep voice.

The youngest one, who couldn't have been more than twenty years old, a real punk kid, with a punk smile, and a really short time left to live, smiled, and said, "The bitch is going down to the meat grinder. From head to toes, she'll be pink meat. Then we'll stuff her in garbage bags and bury her in the desert. It'll be like the bitch never existed. The vultures will--"

Nick leaped across the room and drove two fingers into the man's left eye. Nick felt the cortex squish. He dug his fingers so deep that he gouged a hole in the punk's waste of a brain. The punk went down, jittering his feet and pissing his pants. The punk unleashed a stream of gibberish and drool, and then crashed onto the floor, good and dead.

The other two security goons reached for the pistols from their shoulder holsters. Nick drove a knee into the fatter man's stomach. The goon folded in half like a lawn chair. Nick drove a second knee into the man's nose.

That bloody blow created enough time for Nick to dodge the other pistol about to be pointed at his face. Nick grabbed the gun pointer by the hand and fully extended the security officer's arm.

Then, Nick drove his elbow into the man's elbow and broke the man's arm. Before he unleashed a full shriek, Nick gripped his neck, lifted up his head, and twisted, twisted, twisted, and finally broke the spine/brain stem connection.

"You're dead, you fuck."

Nick dropped the dead man to the floor.

The other security officer crawled across the room and tried to use the coffee table to help him up to his feet. Nick surged across the room. He drove his foot into the side of the man's neck so hard that a shard of bone ripped out the side of his neck. The callous bastard's femoral artery was spraying the floor in spurts of deep red.

This wasn't the King's Suite.

This was Death's Suite.

Nick remembered how the young punk talked earlier. He was full of confidence and misguided youth. Nick had no problem mimicking the dumbass as he spoke into the walkie.

"Hey boss, we had to kick this stupid faggot's ass. We're keeping this no-dick, little pussy under control. Me and the guys just wanted to know if the boss is okay."

Nick recognized Sid's voice. He still sounded like he was still counting the stars circling around his head. "I don't know how the boss is doing. He's holed up in his private office. He won't come out. You just do your job, and I'll do mine, kid. Don't fuck this up. I've heard stories about this Nick Folder asshole. He got the jump on me earlier. It's my fault for underestimating him. Otherwise, I'd be cleaning his skin from the notches of my boots right now."

Yeah, right, asshole.

Anytime.

You and me.

Next time, you'll be dead, you bald fuck face.

"Got it, man. Nick's under control. I'll stomp his ass if he gets out of control."

Sid didn't say anything else.

Nick needed a plan. He had to reach more of Heath's goons. Somebody had to know where Heath Bitterwell's private office was located.

He searched the three security officers for anything useful. He took off his button-up shirt and was only wearing a white undershirt and pants. Nick slung on two shoulder holsters. He was armed with a 9mm under each shoulder. He clutched a Beretta in one hand and a walkie in the other. Nick was ready to make his exit out of the suite when the lights dimmed to half their strength. An intercom clicked on, and an automated voice made a strange announcement.

"THE BUILDING IS NOW ON SECURITY LOCKDOWN MODE. NOBODY IS TO ENTER OR LEAVE THE BUILDING. VIOLATORS WILL BE KILLED."

The automated voice hit Nick with dread.

Something was seriously wrong here.

Nick stormed out of the suite. He used universal precautions, knowing more security would be waiting outside the doorway. What shocked him the most was that the security officers saw Nick coming and put down their guns.

"We don't want any trouble, pal!"

The other blabbered, "This is too fucked up for my taste. I don't want to be in any building that says it can kill me. You win! You win!"

Nick kicked the guns away from them and told them to keep their hands up.

Other suites were opening. Patrons stuck their heads out and peered around the area with frightened expressions. They were talking among themselves and discussing the troubling announcement.

"You got some questions to answer," Nick said to the security persons. "Where is Heath's office?"

"Somewhere on the thirty-fourth floor, but you can't get in without a code. The elevator doesn't stop on the floor without a key card, or a code. I'm not sure about what goes on in there. Probably some fucked up shit I don't want to know about. I'm just not sure about any of it."

Nick pointed at a gun at his face. "Get sure, my friend. Tell me everything."

The other security goon chimed in quick. "Look, my partner's not lying to you. Mr. Bitterwell is really secretive about his affairs. Man, I barely make twenty grand a year before taxes doing this shit. I'm not a criminal. Take my gun. I'm getting the fuck out of here. This ain't worth it."

Patrons from their rooms were crowding around the two security officers and Nick.

They were full of questions.

"What is this nonsense about a security lockdown?"

"Yeah, we were going to go to Freemont Street. You saying if I leave, I'll be killed?"

"You've given my wife and kids the scare of their lives with this stunt, and what's with the dimmed lights?"

"I want to talk to the person in charge."

"We want answers."

"I'll sue!"

"What is the Bitterwell Casino willing to do to make this better? I'm not paying for somebody to threaten my family's life. This is unacceptable."

Fifty people were crowding around Nick and the security officers. The officers tried to shove through them, but the mob mentality was setting in. The customers were angry, and they wanted to be appeased.

Nick would find it funny in another situation.

This wasn't that situation.

The security officers tried to wedge their way through the crowd. No luck. "Let us through. We'll see what's going on, folks. We can't answer your questions standing here in this hallway."

"You're not going anywhere. Call up your boss. I want to talk to him face-to-face."

"Yeah, somebody's got some serious explaining to do. Nobody threatens my family. We're on vacation, for heaven's sake!"

"Hey, I called room service an hour ago. Where's my dinner?"

"How come the phone lines suddenly don't work? I tried to call the police. It's like the phone's dead."

"I don't know about the rest of you, but I'm getting really scared."

Nick was about to say something, anything, to calm everybody. The next announcement only fired up the group's panic.

"EVERYBODY REPORT TO YOUR ROOMS. THIS IS YOUR FIRST AND FINAL WARNING."

The automated voice counted down from twenty seconds.

"Get in your rooms, people," both of the security officers insisted. "Do as it says. We'll figure out what's going on. Everybody's inconvenience will be taken into consideration. Please, if you would return to your rooms, we can access the situation, and you can get back to enjoying yourselves."

"Nobody's telling me what to do!"

"I didn't pay a fucking mint to be pushed around."

"King's Suite. More like Bullshit Suite!"

"I'm not going to be treated like cattle. Do you know how much I make a year?"

"Yeah. Where's the person in charge? I got a real earful for the guy!"

Seventeen, sixteen, fifteen...

DADUM!

The ground suffered a tremor. It sounded like an earthquake. The building was jarred. Series of car alarms blasted from outside, followed up by a collection of police sirens and ambulances. Then the sound of concrete toppling over concrete, and was that machine gun fire from outside? Nick wondered. Choppers flew about the sky. Then the sounds of jets streaming by at the speed of hell.

Nine, eight, seven...

Everybody was unified in his or her concern. Suddenly, the intercom's countdown didn't matter. The commotion outside resembled a war zone.

Nick was about to return to his suite and look out the windows to see the action.

It was too late.

Three, two...one.

"SECURITY LOCKDOWN MEASURE #4371 ENGAGED."

Immediately after the announcement, Nick could only process two things.

Screams and blood.

The Ravager

A monster's thoughts weren't in words. The beast could only process barbaric emotions. What it felt was the pain of being woken from a deep hibernation. The blasting of dynamite in its cave couldn't be ignored. The Ravager's slumber was instantly broken. The explosions jarred old memories. The dynamite sounded just like the meteor show that pounded the earth so many millions of years ago. Ravager remembered seeing its fellow kind reduced to pulp and red smithereens by the rocks falling to Earth. Instinct drew it into the cave. Ravager dug, and dug, and dug, until it couldn't dig anymore. Then the hole caved in on itself, and the Ravager's world went dark.

Things had changed since going into a forced hibernation. Ravager's body had become host to ancient parasites that had snuck beneath its plated skin and fed on its blood. The monster constantly felt their sharp mouths dig into his flesh, and suck, suck, and suck. Ravager itched and wanted to claw off its flesh to make the sensations stop. The beast could hear the tiny mouths break the skin and lap up its life force.

Ravager was helpless against them. That's why being woken pissed it off so much. Sleep was painless. Consciousness was agony.

Another thing, there were strange new sounds in the world. Its hearing was attuned to catch things from hundreds of miles away. The beast knew it could never sleep again until those noises were terminated.

The Ravager, shrouded in a green halo of fire that propelled it over the ocean with jet propulsion, flew across the Pacific Ocean. It hovered over California, and soon, it would reach Nevada.

The monster was a victim of its urges and passions. It was going after the noises that created the sensations of its ears bleeding. The sounds of the eating of its flesh. Those tiny little mouths sucking its lifeblood, the noises were just like the chiming of slot machines. The Ravager would do anything to make those awful sounds stop. Ravager was infantile in its rage, but mighty in its power.

Soon, Ravager would touch down in Vegas, and the devastation would begin.

Heath Bitterwell

Sirens blared. Helicopters surrounded the casino. S.W.A.T. teams were unloading from their vehicles and about to charge their way into the building, and was that the military too? Maybe even the NSA? Heath heard somebody talking from a bullhorn. They were demanding him, Heath Bitterwell, to come out with his hands up. The operation was uncovered. Nick Folder had blown the lid off of everything, and what was that last comment? The United States would hand him over to the cartel, so they could execute him any way they wished.

Heath coughed up another mouthful of blood.

He wasn't sure what he was hearing was for real, and what his damaged brain was creating.

I'm not going down. No, no, no, no. This fight isn't over. I'm only beginning. If I'm going down, it's with a fight. The cartel syndicate entrusted me with their operation. If the government wants to ruin my hard work, they're going to have to pay for it with blood!

Another gong went off in Heath's skull. Nick's punches were like baseball bat swings that could crush bone. Was his left eyelid torn? His jawbone felt loose. Could his mandible bone just...fall off? It sure felt like it could. He was internally bleeding. He sensed blood filling up his torso. The sensation was like fire in his belly. Heath's nose kept bleeding, and bleeding, and bleeding. He spit out a corner of his tongue. Heath had bit it when Nick delivered a wild left hook to his cheek.

Drip, drip, drip, drip, drip.

From his hands, from his nostrils, from the mouth he breathed out of, red kept spattering the carpet inside the elevator. He broke away from Sid, and the rest of the casino's security crew. This was his job, and he was going to do it himself.

Heath had escaped from everybody and stumbled to an elevator.

"Level thirty-four, please."

The automated response from the loudspeaker, "Yes sir, Mr. Bitterwell."

The elevator ticked down to thirty-four, and Heath kept listening to what was happening in the building. He could hear foot soldiers stamp up the stairs to intercept Heath. Armed mercenaries were shoving magazines into high-powered weapons, preparing to blow Heath to shreds. The cartel members staying at the hotel were brandishing daggers, lengths of wire for choking, and the loading of all sorts of high-powered weapons to splatter his brains into kingdom come.

Or so Heath was imagining.

He hacked up more blood and tried to stay on his feet.

The elevator seemed to be moving way faster than it was. Heath clutched the wall to steady himself. A strange floating sensation attacked him. Feeling like he was suffering from a mix of anti-gravity and vertigo, Heath collapsed on all fours. He wretched his guts out. Blood. So much blood. How much red could a man spill before he perished?

Heath would find out, but not before doing the cartels and his casino justice. Nobody was stealing what was kept in the vaults on the thirty-fourth floor. This casino was so much more than a place for stupid people to blow their financial wads. The people would soon see. They sure fucking would.

The elevator stopped. Heath forced himself back up to his feet. Nick had broken Heath's left ankle earlier. He limped ahead, grunting and growling like a madman. Blood drops kept spattering the floor. His cocktail girls heard his approach. They filed out of their waiting room down the hall. When their eyes touched him, they were horrified.

"Mr. Bitterwell...are you okay?"

"My God, what happened to you?"

"Heathy...you're bleeding."

"Let's get you to a doctor."

Heath shoved them all away. "Bitches! All of you! Out of my way! I got things to do!"

He lumbered to the very end of the hall to the steel vault door. Heath punched in the codes, gained access, closed the heavy door behind him, and limped past the thousands of lock boxes to the next door. Heath eventually entered the war room.

Heath knew that ten floors below him, a security operation worked full-time monitoring each floor. Their job was surveillance. Heath's was ensuring the safety of the cartel's finances.

Before he could type in his password into the security's database, he got a call on the walkie sitting on the table next to him.

It was Sid.

"Sir, are you there? Please, pick up. It's important. Our guests are being held hostage in the gaming room. I've also been informed by security that a man named Ray Desanti is in charge of the intruders. Do you know who Ray Desanti is? He's an enemy of the cartel. He's trying to get to the thirty-fourth level. I don't want you worrying about anything. I'm going to kill him for you, sir. You need to get to a hospital, Heath. Heath! If you're there, keep listening. Nick Folder's on the loose, boss. You need to get to the war room. I think it's time, but be careful. Don't use the highest level of protection. This can be contained. Please, sir, don't make that mistake. It's not too late to save the casino. Remember what the highest level can do, sir. You'll kill us all."

Heath didn't hear the rest of Sid's warnings.

One of the security screens displayed CNN. It showed Las Vegas, and the towering behemoth stomping between The Mirage and The Luxor buildings.

Heath felt the concussions of an earthquake, and then the uncouth shrieks of a demon beast. The Bitterwell Casino shifted on its foundations, rocked by the giant's thundering steps.

Blood dripped onto the computer keys as he typed commands into the building's security system. Heath kept hearing the sounds of men banging against the vault's door. Machine guns blasting in the nearby hallways. The warnings from multiple bullhorns commanding Heath to give up the operation. Heath imagined snipers setting up from opposite buildings. Men in black spy outfits scaling the building to sneak in and assassinate him.

You're not taking me in alive.

Heath entered his password on the security interface. This would send a computerized message to the cartel men in charge of re-locating the vault's contents. This would let them know the operation was exposed.

The Bitterwell Casino will stand up to any threat.

Even beast.

Blood was gushing out both of his eyes. Heath felt like he was melting, and so was his sanity. All he could see was the color red.

Heath only meant to put the building on lockdown mode to give the cartels enough time to sneak their goods out of the building before anybody could penetrate their operation. He kept entering his password, and hitting *execute, execute, execute, execute.*

The Bitterwell Casino was put on lockdown mode.

The Bitterwell Casino was put on secure mode.

The Bitterwell Casino was put on battle mode.

The Bitterwell Casino was put on war mode.

War mode.

It's just what Sid Rigard had warned him against doing earlier. If Heath was all there, which he very much wasn't, he would've been more careful. A dying man didn't have much care for double-checking his work.

Heath slipped from the chair from a sudden bout of weakness and   went   unconscious.

Tony Puccini

Tony Puccini's problem? A real bad case of greedy palms. When Tony spotted money, he would take it. It was that simple. If someone didn't want to give up the cash, the fists would fly, and the clips would be emptied, and Tony would collect everything. Once Tony had bloodied his hands and greased his palms over time, people began to fear him. Business was easy that way.

Tony's real problem? He knocked off the wrong people in the cartel. He also shot his mouth off with both barrels, and people didn't like what he had to say. He got cocky. Everyday was a power trip. A snort of cocaine, and this four-time felon, full-time grease ball, full-time knuckleduster, shot up an entire bar after an argument over a bar tab. One of the people that died was Red Panda's sister, Janine.

Big mistake.

If you fuck with Knuckle, the man at the top of the cartel's food chain, consider yourself dead.

In the cartel, either you're on top, or you're on the bottom.

Tony was at the very bottom.

Tony had the best view of the room, being in the worst position of anybody in that room.

He looked out at the crowd in The Gold Room. This was a special party room at The Bitterwell Casino. Cartel members only. The walls, the floor, everything was made of glass with a soft purple color exuding through them. A water fountain was placed in the middle of the room. Five women posed as mermaids on a small island. They were naked, and posed, played, and frolicked with each other as the surrounding tables enjoyed the show, talked business, pleasure, skin, and sin. Women dressed like upper class strippers served drinks. Cartel men and women alike were gearing up for a wild night of gambling, sex, and cutting loose. Blowjobs were given under tables. Other brazen members had sex at the booth seating. Cocaine was cut on tabletops and snorted with rolled up thousand dollar bills. Tony could smell the sex, dirty money, and the reek of power that filled the room.

Tony recognized many of the cartel leaders enjoying themselves. Names popped into his head. Stiff. Hammer. Crusher. Baggs. Grip. Knuckles. Spider. Red Panda. Spreader. Bagger. Ernie "The Choke." Grill.

Knuckles kept giving Tony the killing eye throughout the hours Tony had shared the same room with him. Red Panda couldn't make eye contact. She seemed to be constantly on the verge of tears. Normally, Red Panda was known for her callous rage. Had she changed? It didn't matter to him. He was a dead man. A corpse. His future bed was a pile of dirt and worms. There wasn't a damn thing he could do about it.

What could Tony say to Knuckles and the cartel? Apologize for killing Red Panda's sister when he was so drunk and high that the machine gun in his hand seemed to go off by itself? No good. Once blood was spilled, there was no cleaning it up.

Moreover, seriously, what could Tony say? He was presently gagged, so words weren't a medium for tonight's purposes. Tony couldn't move either. His arms and legs were strapped to a circular piece of wood. The wood was painted up to be a giant dartboard.

Tony was a human dartboard.

Throughout the night, Knuckles gave his best buddies one dart. Wherever they hit on the board, they won so much in cash. If they hit Tony's leg, that was five thousand. An arm, also five thousand. If you hit the lower torso, that was ten grand. The chest, the neck, or the eyes, the player got fifteen grand. The face, Knuckles called it twenty g's. The big prize was Tony's balls. Thirty for each testicle.

Right now, Tony was slowly bleeding out. Eighty darts were stuck about his anatomy. They hadn't touched his eyes. He had a dart in his right testicle. Most of them were in his belly. Two were in the neck. One of his ear lobes were stuck to the board, because Spider had other things on his mind other than Tony, and it involved one of those mermaid girls posing in that water fountain.

Knuckles and Red Panda each threw ten darts at him. It was fun at first, but the two had seen worse violence, and they quickly grew tired of the gimmick.

So Tony remained hung up, arms spread out like Jesus Christ, as he bled and bled.

The intense pain didn't matter soon, because Tony *really* did have the best view of the room. First, Tony saw the giant monster stomp between casinos on the strip through the glass walls. Then the overhead announcements said that the building was in war mode. Whatever that meant. Somebody's fucked up joke. It had to be.

Tony didn't have time to laugh.

The room turned into a massacre.

Giant impaling blades burst through the booth seating and stabbed those sitting. Jutting out of the naked oil paintings of naked women posing in lurid ways, machine gun barrels pierced the canvas to riddle the room's guests with holes. A steel string from one end of the room to the other sliced many of the guests at their bellies, cutting many in half, shearing their tops from their bottoms. The mermaid girls were boiled alive in the fountain, bared down to the bone, by the water that suddenly turned into acid. Many of the cartel's elite were butchered by sledge hammers that sprang from contraptions from the floor and walls, bashing in faces, skulls, and chests with such force the hammers went through the bodies like soft butter.

Nobody could escape. The doors were shut and locked. The windows were blocked by new layers of Plexiglas.

Tony had been shot with four bullets to the midsection. He was very close to being dead. There was one thing that he did get to enjoy before the room went deathly silent. Knuckles bled out at his table. An impaling blade had stabbed him through the table when he was about to take a snort of coke. He was frozen, mid-sniff, with blood gushing from his face.

Tony's greatest enemy was dead.

Tony could rest in peace.

Ray Desanti

"SECURE MODE ENGAGED. BATTLE MODE ENGAGED. WAR MODE ENGAGED."

Ray heard the intercom blast these words. Everybody's apprehension was elevated ten-fold. He wasn't sure if this was some kind of security rouse to scare Ray and his team, but he wasn't buying it.

He would soon learn otherwise.

Every slot machine stopped playing music. Each one shed a deep red color. The lights overhead went dark. The room was cast in pitch black, except for those blaring red slot machines. People started to run for the doors to escape. Ray told his team to hold back. Don't fire. Hold on. It did no good.

Each slot machine spun on their own, as if in play. In tandem, each machine hit its jackpot, and exploded!

Coins were hurled like bullets. Ray hit the deck. He craned his neck in time to see the projectiles pierce through bodies, shredding right through them.

The lights came back on. Hundreds of bodies were bleeding out on the floor. The terror wasn't over. Ray crawled on the ground, refusing to get up. He knew it couldn't be that easy to infiltrate the cartel. This casino was full of tricks and traps. Leave it to men like Heath Bitterwell to come up with something so diabolical.

Those who hid in the restaurants, spas, boutiques, and gift shops, suffered even worse fates. From the overhead lights, the bulbs shattered themselves, then out burst plumes of raging flames. The businesses became hot furnaces of burning death. Unbreakable Plexiglas trapped those inside. People bashed their bodies against the barrier, leaving hunks of boiling flesh stuck onto the plastic. Once those inside cooked long enough, the place was doused in flame retardant foam. Ray gagged on the stench of cooked flesh. Mottled, blackened-to-a-crisp bodies lay gnarled and splayed in disturbing contorted positions.

Up from the floor sprang a Gatling style mini-gun that sprayed bullets in all directions. Thousands of bullets chopped the place into bits and pieces. Chunks of hands, ribbons of flesh, flying gray matter, bits of bones, wet hunks of guts, pulped mess, everybody was reduced to red rags.

The casino patrons were dead.

Ray's team was dead.

He was the only one left alive, except for one other person.

A pile of bullet-ravaged bodies shifted. Beneath the corpses, a man stood up. He was dressed as a casino employee. He didn't have the appearance of a security guard, but instead a higher-level goon in good fighting shape.

The man wiped a hunk of long intestine hanging from his left ear and stood up.

Ray aimed his M-16 at the stranger.

The man held his hands up in surrender. "Whoa, hold on. My name is Sid Rigard. I'm the head of security here. I won't lie. I came down here to kill you. I know who you are, Ray Desanti. I also know why you're here. The thing is, all bets are off. My boss has gone off the deep end. He's engaged the building into war mode. We're not leaving until we can turn it off."

"Then let's go," Ray said, challenging him. "I'll follow your lead, since you know so much. I'll stay right behind you."

Sid gestured frantically with his hands. "I'm unarmed. Can't you see we're all in equal danger? I need your help. This building will be full of traps soon. I need a second pair of eyes to watch my back. I can get into my boss' private room, and flip the switch to turn this shit off.

Heath Bitterwell's got a screw loose. It's a long story, but he's lost his mind, I think. He set this all in motion."

It sounded like cannons and machinegun fire were going off outside. Earthquake tremors rocked the ground. DOOM! DA-DOOM! DOOM!

Ray didn't know what to make of it. "What the fuck is that?"

Sid stepped slowly towards Ray. He removed a phone from his pocket. "May I show you something? We've got yet another problem on our hands. A real *big* problem."

Ray kept the machine gun aimed at the bald asshole. "Okay. Then show me something."

Sid turned the phone so Ray could see the news reports of Vegas being attacked by a creature of mega size. The news broadcasted clips of a giant lizard-beast smashing through the local casinos and hotels.

"That's what's going on out there? Unbelievable. I mean...there's no way this is possible."

Sid agreed. "Yeah, well, it's out there, and the creature is getting closer. We have to turn off the building's security mode, and get the fuck out of here, before we're all squashed."

"That monster will turn this building into a pile of rubble."

Sid agreed. "Yes, but the building's defenses will buy us some time. Only for so long, though."

"What do you mean...the building's defenses? What the hell else can this building do?"

"I'll explain on the way up to the thirty-fourth floor. There's no time. We have to trust each other."

Ray scoffed. "Trust you? Yeah, right."

"I know you, Desanti. You want revenge against the cartel. What you do on the thirty-fourth floor is your business. I only want to survive. There's no point making serious bank working for Bitterwell if you're not alive to enjoy it."

Ray didn't have time to consider his options, because there were none.

He followed Sid.

"We're taking the stairs. Fuck the elevator."

Ray agreed.

They took it on foot to the emergency stairs to reach the thirty-fourth floor.

Nick Folder

Everything went to hell in a flash. That split-second moment offered Nick a short window to save himself. He leaped up off of the floor, grabbed hold of the light fixture on the hallway ceiling, and held on for his life. Below, the fifty-odd guests standing there screaming didn't stand a chance. Once the automated voice announced the building was on war mode, everything was reduced to spurts of blood and horrified screams.

Up from the floor came a grid of red laser-lights. The laser lights chopped off everybody's feet at the ankles. Dozens of the appendages were sent crashing against the walls, deflecting off of each other, and striking the ceiling. Victims landed on the floor with spurting stumps for feet. The irate guests were literally wading in crimson death.

Nick didn't let go of the fixture until the laser lights vanished. He landed on two bodies. Most of them were already dead, stunned by shock, or quickly on their way to death.

Nick had to think. What the hell he was going to do now?

He heard the doldrums of war outside. Blasts of cannons. Machine guns firing angry hell. Emergency sirens spread about the city. War was spreading in here, as it was outside.

The Bitterwell Casino had something seedy going on under its surface. After standing among the hallway full of dead people, he realized something. This was no accident that he was sent here to enjoy a "vacation." This was another assignment from the good ol' United States government. It absolutely had to be.

Bastards.

They never cared about me, and they never will.

Nick only wanted to escape, get a new identity, and escape this horrible life for good. No more missions, and no more bullshit.

Nick treaded through the maze of corpses to the elevator. Before he touched the button, he heard the elevator drop past his floor at incredible speeds. People were screaming inside the death box. Seconds later, he heard a giant crash from the ground floor.

Every where's a death trap.

What the hell kind of hotel is this?

He rushed to the emergency stairs. When Nick stepped down one level, he saw the throng of other guests who had the same idea. The problem, the stairs suddenly collapsed and turned into a downward slide. Guests were sent rolling downwards. Below the slide, an opening in the floor led into a box of mean looking chopping blades.

A meat grinder with hundreds of insane chopping and dicing blades.

Nick dove for the door nearest him and leapt over the threshold. Once the door closed and muffled the sound of grinding bones and liquid mutilation sunk in, a new set of problems presented themselves.

A man was running naked with half his skull melting in the hallway. The woman, who Nick assumed was his wife, was screaming, "*He was just taking a shower! He was just taking a shower! The water melted his face like acid!*"

Nick couldn't stand to watch the man's features be sizzled down to bone any longer. He shot the man dead.

The wife protested, "Why did you do that? How could you? You're horrible!"

At first, it looked like the woman's head was sheared off her neck by an invisible force. Nick caught the source barely in time. The shine of a steel string running from one wall to the other wall flagged his attention. Nick blasted his 9mm until the moving steel string broke.

Safe for now, safe for however long, Nick investigated the area. Many of the rooms' doors were wide open. He imagined whatever system had killed all of these people also opened the doors. Inside a nearby suite, a hot tub was busy with a grease ball looking guy with four women. They were all boiling together. Pieces of flesh were beginning to slouch off their bodies, as they were being cooked so hard.

The television in the room was on. A reporter was speaking in the camera. She was on Freemont Street. "Terror has fallen from the sky. A giant monster has--"

The feed went black.

Nick didn't need the news to tell him what was already happening.

He saw The Ravager punch Harrah's Casino in half.

What in fucking hell is that thing?

The smell of boiling bodies drove Nick out of the room. He stayed at the ready for anything to come his way.

He made one false step. The wood in the floor was splitting. He wasn't sure what was happening until he saw one of the walls disintegrate. Nick saw through to the next room, and the showerhead that kept spraying acid-water. The floor in that room was see-through.

Nick didn't have an opportunity to react. Weakened floorboards cracked and splintered. The weakened structure dropped him down to the floor below him.

He landed in a hotel room where a man and his wife lay in one bed, and two little girls lay in another. Each was in pieces, from the saw blades that had sprung from the mattresses and delivered death.

Nick couldn't believe his eyes.

He launched out of the room, and into another hallway, sharp poles were stabbing down from the ceiling. Many victims already had holes poked into their skulls, while the smarter people lay on the ground cowering in fear. Nick wasn't sure what he could do for them, so he said to stay where they were at, and to wait for help to arrive.

Nick knew his words didn't reassure them one iota.

He thought he was safe by staying low when the sharp steel poles suddenly sprang from the floor. One man got the pole right up his ass and out the top of his head. Another had her leg punched through so many times it severed the appendage from her hip.

Nick dodged the poles, and carefully treaded towards the emergency exit door. He managed to open it without anything happening to him.

Others already in the emergency stairwell didn't fare so well.

From above, the victims were still being meat grinded from earlier. Below, those stampeding against each other were scooped up by a net. Odd, Nick thought, seeing how the fabric of the net reflected light like steel. The people were wrapped up in the net and dangled up high above that section of the stairway. Nick couldn't help but feel anguish for them, as they reached out to him and begged for help. He unloaded a series of 9mm shots from the slot in the wall that had unleashed the net. It did no good.

The net started to heat up like an oven coil. So hot that the coils sliced through the bodies. Body parts rained down the stairway. By the time the pieces reached the bottom floor, the people were battered slop.

Nick raced down the stairway while the net was doing its work. He dared to peer over the edge of the thirty-odd levels in the staircase. Nick could only see blood and human limbs spray. God knows what contraptions were the culprits of their slaughter.

There was no escape, up or down.

Nick really had to think if he wasn't going to be turned into unrecognizable matter. Upstairs, amounted to death. Downstairs, amounted to death. Everywhere, death, death, death.

He had one idea.

He clutched a 9mm in each hand after he made his decision.

Nick wouldn't be using the stairs at all.

Chopper Dan

The pilot did his best to keep his eyes open. He was dying, and his body told him in every way possible that he would only stay alive for a matter of hours. What did keep him awake, and fighting through the pain, was tracking the beast. Maybe Chopper Dan himself hadn't woken the demon in that mountain, but he wasn't going to let innocent people die because of someone else's mistake.

Chopper Dan had been flying for hours. He kept listening to the radio. The creature hadn't attacked any other places. It had a destination in mind, and just now, over the radio, it was announced that the creature landed in Las Vegas.

Landed was an understatement.

Chopper Dan did his best to communicate with the military in the air, the forces on the streets, and even the local Las Vegas police. He couldn't get through to anybody.

They didn't know the monster's weakness.

Damn it all! Why doesn't anybody answer my calls?

Somebody finally did.

Kathy Ingrid.

"Kathy? Oh, it's great to hear your voice. Have you been able to contact anybody, and tell them what I told you about that monster?"

"I've been shut out," Kathy said, venting her frustration. "I guess the President has allowed all forces to go in and try to obliterate the beast. So far, we're getting our asses kicked. Nobody can even slow the monster down. It was reported when it flew over the Raider's game in Oakland that it took a shit on the stadium. The fans, the stadium, were all buried in monster shit. The crowd drowned in fucking shit."

"Holy fuck," Dan said, in shock. "I can only imagine what else it has done to other cities. This is a hopeless situation. I guess I have to go in myself, and take care of business. Nothing changes. You give the assholes the obvious answer, and they refuse to take the easy way out. So many people are going to die in Las Vegas, and if we don't kill that monster..."

"Don't say that," Kathy said. He could hear the peril in her voice. "Everybody's counting on you, Dan. You want a bit of incentive? The second you destroy that monster, you're going to land, and we're getting you to the hospital."

"I won't make it that long," Chopper Dan admitted. "I've got about an hour before I reach Las Vegas. I'm bleeding internally."

"I've got another incentive."

He winced through a violent wave of abdominal pain. "What would that be?"

"You get a date with me."

"Is that right?" He couldn't help but smile. "Could you handle a date with a jerk loser like me?"

"You're not a loser," Kathy laughed, "maybe a jerk, but you're not a loser."

"That means everything, hearing you say that."

"One other thing, Chopper Man."

"Yeah?"

"When I'm at the news desk giving my reports, you were right. I don't wear panties. I tend to do the same on dates. Remember that, Dan. Seriously. I want you to live, and I want you to kill that fucking monster."

"Don't you worry," Dan said with a new determination. "Ravager is as good as dead. You'll be the first to report it, Kathy Ingrid."

Ray Desanti

Ray watched Sid throw open the emergency exit door. Sid was immediately thrown back by a thick tide of blood. Ray helped the man back up to his feet. They both stood there in shock as the wave of blood thinned out along the game room floor. Once they collected themselves, Sid propped the emergency exit doors open. Along each step, steel prongs had stuck through fifty-odd people. The victims were propped up like puppets, the steel stuck up their backs, or through their asses, to keep them forced in a standing position. Blood was trickling down from higher up floors. Horrible screams echoed from other sections of the building.

"Don't worry," Sid said, "the system is designed to kill intruders."

"Oh, that's a relief!"

Ray wasn't sure what to make of the head of building security. He was as evil and corrupt as the cartels he aimed to rob today.

"No, I mean the system will recognize my voice," Sid said. "You stay with me, watch my back, we'll both get out of here alive. *On one condition.*"

Ray scoffed. "We can't buddy up without a condition. I should've seen it coming."

"Hey, asshole," Sid growled, "you came in here, blew out the back door, and came in here with a bunch of people with machine guns. You're as much of a bad guy as I am. Now listen to me, you used to work for the cartel, or did you forget? You came here to steal cartel money. We're all bad guys. Get over it.

"My condition, if you'll hear me out, you forget what you came here to do. You watch my back, you help me turn off this insane security system from hell, and we'll part ways. That simple."

Ray knew he couldn't trust the bald asshole. Nobody can be trusted in organized crime. Ray understood Sid couldn't trust him either, but what choice did he have? Sid knew more about this building that could kill people than Ray did. Ray was simply at the mercy of his enemy.

"We part ways. That's a deal."

They shook on it.

"Tell me something," Ray asked, "why rig a casino to do all of this shit? It's pretty sadistic."

"You said it," Sid said, studying the inside of the emergency exit door, checking the angles, and thinking something over with painful scrutiny. "The cartels teamed up with Heath Bitterwell to build a casino that would double as a safe house for every drug cartel, local and abroad. Drugs, money, dead bodies, evidence, anything, can be stored here for safe keeping. Money can easily be laundered through this cash cow of a casino.

"If somebody, including the DEA, tried to overtake this place, the cartels wanted to send a message to all of its enemies that if you fuck with the cartels, you die horribly, and so do innocent people. It's all about creating a culture of fear.

"It's a long story how this got started, but Heath Bitterwell himself got into a serious altercation with a guest earlier. The guy beat up Heath to the point the man was probably on his way to brain damage, or death. So Heath runs to the security room that controls the casino's special defense abilities.

"Heath must be out of his mind, or delusional, after having his brain beat to mush, because he must think the operation's at the highest level of danger. It doesn't help that there's a giant fucking monster stomping around out there. Heath freaked the fuck out, end of story. This building wasn't supposed to turn into a killing box unless ALL shit hit the fan. Well...I guess all shit hit the fan, and now we're on war mode."

Ray listened to both Sid's words, and the sounds of battle raging on outside. "So how do we get out of here?"

"The security system is rigged to recognize the sound of my voice. I keep talking, identify myself, and you stay with me, we should be fine. We have to reach the thirty-fourth floor. That's where Heath is hiding, if he's still alive. I know the codes to get into his security room. I'm not supposed to. We turn off the system, and we use the secret elevator to escape."

"Secret elevator?"

Sid paused, unsure if he should tell him about the elevator.

"By now, somebody's been called to round up the money, drugs, and everything stored in the vaults on the thirty-fourth floor. The cartel uses a private elevator to reach the thirty-fourth floor. Then there's an underground tunnel leading to a secured location, where everybody can make a fast getaway with the goods."

Ray liked what he was hearing. The cartel boys would be moving fast and frantic to gather up their money and illegal items. That would be his time to strike. Sid probably had the same thing in mind against him.

So be it, Ray thought. What choice did he have?

Sid spoke at the emergency exit. "I'm Sid Rigard. Head of security at The Bitterwell Casino. I'm here with my associate."

An automated voice spoke. "*Access granted.*"

Sid took the first steps, filing between the impaled bodies on the stairs. Ray quickly followed. They both prayed the security system didn't turn on them.

Ravager

Ravager screeched, stomped, growled, and threw its head back as it unleashed its torment. Those awful sounds. Like the chirping of death.

The infernal slot machines!

The beast had traveled for hundreds of miles, and now it touched down on the Las Vegas strip. Daylight was limited to a purple backdrop of color. The casinos lit up what would soon be full-on night. The flashing lights, the sounds of slot machines, of music, it sent the monster into a rage.

The Ravager would have his revenge.

Then it could finally sleep in peace again.

The   reptile-beast-behemoth-juggernaut-volatile-hideous-monster balled up its fist. Its travels made it so hungry. It stood between the Flamingo and Excalibur casinos to catch its breath. Below, hundreds of citizens were scampering for their life.

Hungry, Ravager's mouth gaped open. Lashing its long tongue like a whip, the tongue extended three blocks along a sidewalk. The tongue was covered in a sticky substance, and the screaming crowds were like flies on flypaper. Like a frog, its tongue retracted back into its mouth. Over two hundred screaming people were swallowed up in its maw and instantly dissolved by advanced stomach acid.

Ravager's bulging eyes burned a brilliant crimson.

Ravager saved up its breath, let its rage build, build, build, and then it screamed at the MGM Grand. The gold lion in front of the glass skyscraper was blown off its perch and smashed through the building. Screaming harder, screaming with increasing verve, glass and steel were dismantled by the insane blast of air.

The MGM was there one moment, and then gone the next.

Ravager, sparked up by the scene of destruction, used both fists to mash, punch, level, and squash The Bellagio into ruins. The Bellagio was reduced to ruins, as if it was a mere popsicle stick house.

The sounds of the slot machines didn't stop.

So grating, Ravager couldn't stand it.

From the air, air assault aircrafts from every angle delivered a front of missile and machine gun fire. One rocket pounded Ravager between the shoulder blades. Shards of his plated back littered the streets below, freeing up hundreds of mites, plated creatures, and ancient parasites that didn't waste a moment stalking the fleeing citizens on the streets below.

Ravager didn't let another bullet or rocket touch him. Tensing up its muscles, Ravager's green halo spread around its body. The halo absorbed the rockets and bullets. Ravager used that energy before the force could consume its body and projected it out of its body. From beneath its tongue, the Ravager sprayed jets of boiling acid at the air fleet surrounding him. The air assault fleet was rendered into dissolving steel as they crashed down into the city.

The adrenaline junkies enjoying the Skyjump, Bigshot, X-Scream, and Insanity thrill rides on the rooftop of the Stratosphere Casino were the next victims. The Ravager swatted the rides and the people enjoying them with one claw's swipe. Roller coaster cars catapulted off the track in pieces, as did the patrons. The Ravager screamed at the rest of the building, and it erupted as if raised by dynamite.

Dozens of tanks blasted at the monster from the streets. More aerial attacks were on the way. From rooftops of nearby casinos, artillery cannons were being set up to blast the enemy. The green halo absorbed every shot taken at the Ravager. The halo turned into an even brighter ultraviolent neon green. The Ravager opened up its arms, and out burst the green colors onto the streets, and up into the sky. The green produced a higher degree of fire. The green flames were enough to melt the skin and muscle from human bodies instantly, and turn steel into crumpled up, useless masses.

The first stand against the Ravager was a failure.

The Ravager still heard those infernal slot machines playing their disconcerting music.

The beast continued to smash through the nearby buildings. It wouldn't stop until everything was rendered silent, and maybe then, the monster could finally sleep in peace once again.

Nick Folder

Nick's 9mm's chewed holes into the stairway wall, shredding it up like paperboard. He emptied two clips before kicking through to the other side. Reason would dictate after seeing insane weapons sprout from the stairs, something interesting had to be going on inside the walls. He prepared himself for any kind of security backlash.

When Nick bent through the hole and crawled inside, there was a narrow passage that channeled upwards. A stepladder led up to each floor. He had trouble seeing too much in the darkness, but he did see blinking lights from mechanical processes, along with electrical wires channeling from metal box to metal box.

Nick had to stare really hard at the wall to understand what he was viewing in the dark. He imagined a giant gun clip. Bullets the size of small missiles were stored in steel housings. Was this to load something else in the building?

He tried to wrap his mind around the enigma, and just couldn't. Nick kept trying, though. Down further, Nick noticed more openings in the walls. Places for metal arms to be folded up, waiting to be deployed. Sheets of glass. Fuel to create fire. Steel poles posed to slide under the stairs and punch through the steps to kill. Barrels marked with skull and crossbones. Poisons and acids. The walls stored a bank of tools for slaughter.

Nick decided to take a risk. He was guaranteed dead if he used the stairs to get anywhere, but within the walls, Nick might stand a chance.

He had to reach the thirty-fourth floor.

Nick used the ladder and began his descent.

The Removal Team

Graziano lead the team of fifteen from an elevator that could be reached from a sewer connection secretly built under The Bitterwell Casino. This would take them straight to where they needed to be. The team was dressed in black, and wearing gas masks in case they had to go in spraying tear gas. They were heavily armed with M-16's and AK-47's. Shit could get real, real fast, knowing the amount of money, supplies, evidence, and personal items belonging to the cartel that was stashed up in The Bitterwell Casino's thirty-fourth floor. Once the elevator opened up, they were right inside the vaults. The elevator was triple wide to accommodate their job of removal.

They dragged in a long push cart.

Graziano directed everybody.

"Break up into five groups of three. Cover each wall. The lock boxes automatically unlocked once we stepped foot on that elevator. Pile the lock boxes in organized fashion. I don't want to see crooked stacks. We need to clean this place out efficiently. We have five minutes to get the job done. Now get going!"

The team worked double-quick. Graziano monitored everybody's progress. In that small window of time, the seasoned cartel man knew of many other operations similar to The Bitterwell Casino that were hubs for money laundering and cartel safe houses. Never once had he experienced something like this where the building had slaughtered hundreds, if not thousands of people. On top of that, the wild beast that was stomping outside added another surreal element to the night's already crazy feel.

Graziano was terrified of the sounds of machine gunfire outside. Military, police, any force the government could muster, would be working outside to stop that monster. He wouldn't have a have a hard time finishing his job in here, Graziano thought, but once they were out of this building, and back out on the streets, and possibly face-to-face with that monster, there was no gun big enough, or car fast enough, truly to protect them.

The team had cleaned out the slots in the vault in five minutes flat.

"Move your asses people. We're going down. If we fuck this up, the big bosses will chop you up into little pieces and send your pieces to your families, postage due."

The team knew what was at stake. Everybody worked together to push the heavy cart into the elevator. Once inside, Graziano hit the button to the sub-level. When they reached that floor, before the doors opened, they could hear something that didn't sound...quite right. Scratching. Masticating. Hissing.

Graziano told the team to arm themselves right before the doors opened.

Ray Desanti

Gore soaked the stairways on each floor. Ray worked with Sid to make sure nothing sprang out to murder them. The weapons used on the victims were gone. Only the eviscerated corpses, mutilated, burnt, and slaughtered messes remained. Sid kept identifying himself as the head of security to the automated system. The plan seemed to be working. They were making fast progress, and now, they were standing outside the door to enter the thirty-fourth floor.

Sid gave the orated tour. "This floor has guests quarters. They're fake rooms. A private elevator brings Heath to his security office. On this floor, you have to go through several secret rooms to gain access to where we need to be."

Ray listened as they entered the thirty-fourth floor. His eyes kept widening at what he saw in the hallways. As they moved past each room, blood pooled from the floorboards of each room. Ray didn't want to know what had befallen them.

Sid slid a key card into one of the rooms. When they entered, nobody was inside. There was no furniture, or amenities. Only an empty box. That room had yet another security door. Sid slid the key card, and they gained entry.

"This is one complex casino," Ray said. "The cartels really didn't want anybody standing in their way."

"It wasn't supposed to be like this," Sid said. "If Heath was of the right mind, he wouldn't have engaged war mode."

The building shook. Wild quaking made the two men hold onto the walls so they wouldn't be pitched onto the floor. More sounds of gunfire and buildings collapsing followed. Constant chaos was at a constant.

"Even if we make it out of here," Ray said, "I'm not sure it'll be any better out there."

Sid checked his phone for updated news feeds. "The military is trying to fight that giant thing out there. It looks like they're losing the fight."

"So how do we get out of this place?"

"A private elevator takes us underground. The elevator goes to a sub-level where there are vehicles, supplies, and the right equipment to move everything in the cartel's secret vault to a new location. People are already at work emptying the vaults."

Ray realized he was in the perfect position really to damage the cartel. He imagined burning their money, emptying their electronic bank accounts, and sending the cartel into financial ruin.

Sid's walkie went off at his hip. He answered it. "Rigard here. What's going on?"

A weak, pain-choked voice spoke. "There was no way to protect them. Everybody inside The Gold Room is dead, and so am I. Escape if you can."

The communication was terminated.

"Who was that?" Ray asked.

"One of the guards who protect the special party room for the cartel big wigs. You'll be happy to know they're all dead. That's what you came here to do, right?"

"That's not all," Ray said. "I had other plans."

"I know you did," Sid growled, "and you won't be taking a single penny. That's rightfully mine! I've been a bitch for the cartel for too long!"

Before Ray could swing his machine gun at Sid, Sid removed a Glock from his ankle holster and delivered a bullet up through Ray's jaw and out the back of his head.

Ray crumbled to the floor.

Dead.

"Your enemies are dead, friend," Sid said, stepping over Ray's corpse and entering the final room leading to Heath Bitterwell's private quarters. "*But the money is all mine*."

Fodder

Gary Blackwell was pumping quarter, after quarter, after quarter into the slot machine. He heard the screams, and the terror spread outside. Gary didn't care. He really didn't. He'd lost every penny at the Riviera crap table today. People had abandoned their plastic cups of coins when they fled the scene. He used those coins to play. Gary was going to win that money back, and on the Lucky 7's machine, he was now on a shot streak. Gary stayed glue to the chair even when every floor above him was leveled down on top of him when The Ravager jumped up and slammed both legs down to smash the building like a tin can.

S.W.A.T. team leader Erin Larson couldn't see shit. There was dust from toppled buildings spreading everywhere. Up the street, everything was obscured by the haze. The haze itself was dirt, glass, and something that smelled like dead fish.

Larson commanded his team to wait. Nobody was to fire his or her weapons until there was more visibility.

Larson could hear his men's buttholes clench, unclench, and clench yet again. Jets streaked above in the sky. Larson caught the beast chomping down on one jet. The jet blew up in its mouth, and the monster casually spit it out as if it had bit into a ghost chili pepper.

The monster was tensing up its body, flexing its arms, straightening its spine, and when it was done, a brilliant neon green aura brightened the night sky.

The dark haze was lifted. By the power of the green light, Larson and his S.W.A.T. team could see the legion of unbelievable creatures approach them. He imagined crawdads mixed with ants, beetles crossed with lobsters, sharks crossed with horse flies, and maggots crossed with centipedes. They were plated, designed to devour, and hungry as hell. Hundreds of the ugly horde challenged the S.W.A.T. team.

Larson didn't have to give the order. The men blasted their M-16's, riot guns, 12-gauges, and even hurled grenades into the stampede.

Larson's team didn't stand a chance.

They were devoured in minutes.

NSA member Chuck Holiday and his team watched Larson's crew be chewed up by clicking mandibles, sucking worm mouths, and hands that cracked bodies like hungry patrons eating crab legs at a seafood joint.

Military forces were backing up Holiday's group with tanks, foot soldiers, and choppers up in the sky. The bullets, the missiles, the monster's stomping, shrieking, and pulverizing glass and steel were a constant soundtrack to the deadly battle.

Hails of bullet fire pulped the sea bugs. Green puss, yellow insides, and steaming entrails even a scientist couldn't identify were splattered against the streets. Tanks blasted the intimidating throng of monsters into a boiling street bouillon. Military Jeeps armed with M-60's spattering machine gun fire turned the plated beasts into something coughed out of a garbage disposal. The final nail was the bold team of NSA who planted a row of Claymores. The orange bursts mixed with the Ravager's green aura created a new ultraviolet death color.

Holiday thought they had won the battle, but the NSA, the leftover S.W.A.T., local police, firefighters, and military had no idea who was watching over their shoulders.

STOMP. STOMP. STOMP.

HUFF.

Hrrrrrrrrrrrrrrrrrrrrrrrr.

Ravager towered above the squads in the streets. It bent forward, extended its head, and unleashed a scalding bath of puke. Everything was vaporized instantly in a boiling concoction of putrid super death.

Can't this thing be stopped?

Shit, I don't know.

Ace pilot, Bryce Kramer, guided the stealth fighter plane down the burning Las Vegas strip. Chaos was an understatement. Those betting on winning big in this town had become instant losers.

What's this big bitch doing now?

After vomiting on the forces on foot, Ravager ran full speed and did a Superman jump and landed belly first onto of the Palazzo casino. Glass shot out both sides of Ravager's body as the crushing force of its body easily toppled the building.

When the beast got up, picking glass, the steel rails jutting out of its body, and a Planet Hollywood sign stuck under its right armpit, Ravager's enormous eyes seemed to make direct contact with Kramer's jet.

You targeting me, bitch?

Bring it!

A voice blared on Kramer's radio. He heard a voice try to break in on his frequency.

"...much time left. You have to shoot this monster in the--"

The frequency cut out before Kramer made sense of who was speaking. Kramer knew what he had to do. He was out of missiles.

Kramer prayed to God.

Then he tripled his speed.

"I'm going to crash right into your FACE!"

Ravager reared back its head, opened its hideous mouth, and lashed his tongue at the stealth fighter and blew Kramer out of the sky.

Gertrude Beeman, an eighty-five year old armed with a purse stuffed with the eight hundred dollars she won from playing penny slots for six hours at Caesar's Palace, and a can of mace, stood beside an expired parking meter. There was no more Vegas strip. Only the mangled frames of skyscrapers, tall piles of broken concrete, glass, and brick. The dust was far from settling. She could only see empty streets, ruined cars, and so many mutilated body parts.

She couldn't keep her eyes off of the towering monster that was stomping away from her position. Before a new gathering of mutant mites could pluck Getrude's arms and legs from her body, devour her skin, suck her blood, and smash her ripped off head onto the curb, she noticed one casino was still standing. The bright pillar shined of gold and glass against the fires burning down the block.

The Bitterwell Casino was the only casino remaining in Las Vegas, and the Ravager was headed right for it.

Nick Folder

Nick had ascended down the ladder in the wall to the point his arms and legs were trembling. Exhaustion was setting in. It didn't make the climb any easier hearing the sounds of a losing war being waged outside. The jets, the tanks, the machine gun fire had abruptly ended. Even the beast's battle cries had stopped. There only remained the resounding steps of the beast. The steps were coming closer, and getting louder, with every passing second.

If he didn't get out of this building, he was in trouble.

Nick realized there were so many flaws in his plan. Even if he did find Heath, they would both die when the building was smashed to pieces by that beast. His emotions were all over the place. He kept imagining Audra shot in the head. How many other innocent lives were lost today, inside and outside of this casino? Too many to count.

He made a mistake.

Nick could do a better job getting even with Heath, and whomever he worked for, by surviving this night and investigating Heath Bitterwell and his business dealings.

The government had stuck him in this position from the beginning. He was an unwitting plant. Nick bet they had no idea what this casino could really do, and the monster that would have its hand in wrecking their plan.

The joke was on everybody at this point, he thought, and the punch line?

Death.

It's about time you got your head on straight, pal. You won't settle things with Audra's death by getting yourself killed in this place.

Nick tried to think about how to escape the building when he heard something that changed everything.

Sobbing.

It echoed from the wall across from his position on the ladder. The wall was full of bullet holes. He hadn't heard another person that was alive for at least an hour.

He had to help whoever it was, Nick decided. Something positive had to result from this night of mass death. Even if in doing so, he guaranteed himself to be in this building when that monster came around to smash this casino.

Nick pursued the person in distress.

Sid Rigard

What a stupid piece of shit! You're dead and bleeding on the floor, Ray. You didn't see it coming, did you? That's why that cartel gunned you down in the desert, huh? You're a fucking idiot. You deserve nothing more than to be twitching and bleeding in a puddle of your own brains. People like you, Ray, belong in a body bag, and people like me...belong in a fucking mansion with a pair of babes sucking my gold-covered cock.

Sid had planned for the right moment to steal enough money from the cartel to disappear. He knew the right people who could give him a new identity, and a proper cover story to fall into the life of a stinking rich successful businessman. All he had to do was catch up with the people who had emptied the vaults that were just behind the door he was opening.

He entered the hallway behind the fake hotel room's door. There was blood slathered on the walls in all directions. That was no surprise.

Sid covered his ass. "Sid Rigard. Head of building security."

"*Access granted.*"

The automated voice meant he was safe.

The blood was from the cocktail girls, who hadn't fared so well. Sid could picture the stupid bitches stumbling out of their break room with their collagen-injected lips curled in terror, and their implant-stuffed chests breathing in and out in panic. The laser beams had sliced them from head to toe in a wild show of mutilation. Cross sections of heads, breasts, feet, and emptied torsos were spread out on the ground.

Sid even had to take a moment to collect himself.

The massacre was nasty.

The look in their eyes was the hardest thing to process.

Sid headed towards the security door that led to the war room. He unlocked the locks, used the correct passwords, and he reached the area where the vault slots were emptied. The place had been ransacked in a hurry.

A hidden wall had shifted, showing a secret elevator. That would lead to a safe sub-level, where, if Sid was lucky, he could catch up with the people transporting the items, and steal the money that was about to be moved elsewhere for safe keeping.

Sid entered a side room with code key. The room was full of food items, liquor, and enough guns to protect a paranoid old man if he thought forces were trying to steal what he protected here in these vaults.

He left the room with two Uzis, five grenades, and a 12 gauge strapped to his back with a ream of ammo. Sid entered the secret elevator, hit the button for the sub-level, and imagined himself stacking the fat cash he was about to steal from the unsuspecting cartel mules working downstairs.

Sid didn't believe in luck, as many did in Vegas.

He did believe in crime, however.

Nick Folder

The cries didn't stop. Nick knew they were coming from right behind the bullet-tattered wall. Nick peered through the holes. He spied torn up booths, a bar set-up that was all smashed glass, and a water fountain heaped with dead naked female bodies. Nick's eyes adjusted more to the darkness of the room. He noticed the two or three dozen well-dressed persons mutilated, shot up, and chewed up by God knows what.

Nick saw the woman who was alone against the wall. She was sitting with her knees up against her body. She wore a skimpy black top and short red skirt with red fishnets. The woman had long, died red hair that was in greasy strands, covered in the blood of too many people to count. The only reason he could see her at all was that through the window, the bright red eye of the beast peered into the building. The woman screamed at the sight.

Nick jumped off of the ladder and used his body to power through the weak wall. He landed inside the room, and yelled at the woman, "Come on, let's get out of here!"

Everything in the room was a fiery red color.

When the monster's eyes stopped peeking into the room, everything went dark again. Nick had to blink the amazing light out of his eyes. The woman ran right to him, her high heels clicking against the wet tiles. When she reached Nick, the monster outside unleashed a rip-roaring shriek.

"*Raaaaaaaaaaaaaaaaaaaaaatch*!"

The glass along the walls split and cracked.

"Let's get away from the windows," Nick said. "I don't want that thing seeing us. It's already worked up enough. That monster's unbelievable."

The woman was trembling in his arms. "Okay. Anything you say. Please, just don't hurt me. I can't stand to see any more death.

I never wanted to hurt people. They, they made me for years. They...turned me into something I'm not."

Nick Folder understood what this room had been. There were cartel members splattered on the floor. She was the only survivor. The girl was younger, maybe mid-twenties, early thirties. Nick could see how the events in this room, and the chaos outside, and seeing that giant red orb eye ogle her through the window had shown her the error of her ways.

"Stay with me," Nick said. "I only know if we can reach the thirty-fourth floor, we can turn off the security system, and--"

The intercom spoke, and this time, it wasn't an automated voice.

It was the voice of Heath Bitterwell. The son-of-a-bitch sounded like he was on the brink of death. Heath was all creaks, groans, and wispy gasps.

"*I see you, Nick Folder, and you've made a new friend. It's good to see you, Red Panda.*"

Red Panda? Nick thought. *The hell kind of a name is that?*

Nick processed the girl's crazy black eyeliner, and her red hair, red stockings, and red skirt, and he imagined a red panda...juiced up on sex.

"I'm turning off the building's security system temporarily. Go to the stairway."

The automated voice spoke overhead. "The Bitterwell Casino is now on safe mode."

"*I know you don't trust me, and with good reason,*" Heath continued. "*I'm almost dead because of you, Nick Folder. I should wish death ten-fold upon you, but what I really want to die is that monster outside. I worked so hard to build this casino. I want it to be the only surviving building in Las Vegas. Come up to my security room...and help me destroy that ugly son-of-a-bitch. Hurry...before it's too late.*

"*If granting a dying wish isn't enough for you...which I know isn't enough for you, Nick, then think about the people in danger in this city. This building can stop the monster...if utilized to its maximum efficiency. Believe me, and come up to the thirty-fourth floor, and every door will be open for you. Don't believe me, you stay where you're at, I'll put this building in lockdown mode...and you'll die here along with me, and God knows how many other innocent people will die because you didn't take a chance. Come on, Nick. Kill the monster.*"

That ended the man's message.

Nick wasn't sure about Heath's instructions. The man wasn't dead after undergoing the beating of a lifetime. Either the man had a screw loose and didn't know what he was saying, or he was so proud of his building, he wanted to protect his legacy, or, he was just plain insane.

Nick thought about how he met the grease ball downstairs when he first arrived at the hotel, and how the smug bastard went on and on about how The Bitterwell Casino was magnificent. The man staked everything on this building.

Nick decided he had to take a gamble of his own. The dice were as heavy and deadly as grenades, but he was going to give them a toss across the table, regardless.

"We're going up," Nick said, "it's our only chance."

"But the traps!"

"He shut them off. And think about it, we have no other way of escape. That monster is stomping around outside. We got minutes, maybe only seconds, before we're squashed where we stand. You take a chance, and maybe live, or you take no chance, and absolutely die."

"I want to disappear off the face of the earth," Red Panda said, bursting into desperate tears. "I've wanted out of the cartel for years. They pulled me in when I was only fourteen. I was a drugged out, failed actress, whoring myself out, when Knuckles found me, made me his woman, and I've watched people get killed over drugs and money, and I've killed over drugs and money too. I never wanted to hurt anybody. I only...want to start over again."

"Me too," Nick said. "We have a lot more in common than you think. I'm on the other side of the law. The government's made me their killing puppet for too long. We both make it out of here together, then we'll become new people together. I know how. Come with me, help me, and I'll disappear with you."

STOMP.

STOMP.

STOMP.

The beast was lurking. Too much was happening too fast. It was making Red Panda dizzy. "Anything you say. Like I have any choice. It's pretty clear. Die this way, or die that way. I'm dying no matter what I do. So sure, you've got yourself a deal."

"One question," Nick said, "why do they call you Red Panda?'

Red Panda's piercing eyes met Nick's. "Because I've got a tattoo of a red panda in a place you'll never see."

"Fair enough."

Nick guided her out of the cartel slaughter room and to the emergency stairs.

They headed right up to the thirty-fourth floor.

Sid Rigard

Sid clutched both Uzis as he descended down to the secret sub-level of the casino. He would catch the group off-guard, blast the cartel members to ribbons, and take whatever transport full of fat cash there was and drive off into the sunset. He imagined himself drinking tequila out of a hooker's navel in Mexico, while another bitch serviced his rod. He might take Heath's example, and swig back a shot of stinging hard liquor and go down on one of the bitch's just to hear them squeal.

He removed images of the high life, of easy cash, easier women, and liquor abound from his mind and replaced them with bullet-ridden, pulped bodies. All he had to do was spill some blood, and then he could fill up his wallet.

Right before the elevator door opened, he noticed something strange. Along the bottom crack of the elevator door, he noticed a partially chewed human finger.

Oh...fuck.

There was wild scratching at the door. Then ticks, clicks, chirps, and whistles.

"Noooooooooooooooooo!"

Sid punched the emergency stop button. "Close, damn you, close!"

The door opened a few inches, then was about to close, when the horde of plated insect/crustacean's stuck their bodies through the opening. Feelers, stick arms, ant-heads, crab-bodies, and plated maggots all invaded the elevator.

Sid caught the open area beyond the incoming throng of monsters. The cartel goons were spread out in a small parking lot, their bodies being hollowed out of meat and tasty bits. Hundreds, and hundreds, and hundreds of the creatures were charging at the elevator.

Sid spread Uzi-fire all around. The barking machine guns might as well have been cap guns. A lobster pincher matched with a praying mantis's long arms seized the guns and bent them into useless pieces.

When Sid reached for his grenades, dozens of mandibles and hungry mouths flensed Sid's body to the point he was only a standing, screaming skeleton, in mere seconds.

Nick Folder

Nick and Red Panda made their way up the emergency stairs. Once they reached the thirty-fourth floor, they entered a new hallway. This area didn't have nearly as many heaps of gore and death as the other floors. Red Panda had trouble holding back her gorge during the trip.

"Hang in there," Nick said, "I'm going to get you out of here."

Heath's voice spoke over the intercom. *"Go to room 237. I'll open it for you."*

Nick did so, seeking out the room. Once they entered 237, they realized it was an empty room. Heath then told them to go into the side door. The door unlocked itself, and Nick and Red Panda were in yet another empty hotel room.

They found a corpse sprawled on the ground.

The man had his brains blown out of his head.

The door in front of the dead man unlocked itself. When Nick opened it, they entered a new hallway. Nick shielded Red Panda from the half-naked dead women splattered on the floor. Heath told them to walk beyond the walls featuring hundreds of empty slots. The place looked to have been a room of bank boxes. Two more doors unlocked themselves, and they entered a well-furnished room that stank of piss, blood, and cigar smoke.

Nick raised his 9mm up at Heath sitting in a chair that faced a giant wall of security screens. Every screen showed rooms of death, heaped stacks of bodies, and the death and destruction The Bitterwell Casino's security system had perpetrated.

Heath turned in his chair. The man was slumped forward. One arm clutched his belly with a sharp grimace of pain on his face. The other arm was balancing a cigar. His face was covered in dried blood, while new blood continued to ooze from both nostrils, the sides of his mouth, and out of his left ear. Heath's face looked like a meat-tenderized slab of raw meat.

Nick growled, "What now, Bitterwell?"

Mr. Bitterwell coughed, and then he tightened his arm over his belly. "I'm bleeding internally that's what now, you fucking son-of-a-bitch."

"You wanted me up here so you can kill me?" Nick pressed the dying man. "I got this 9mm pointed right at your ugly face. I die, so do you."

"I'm dead anyway," Heath said. "If you saw those empty bank slots outside this room, you'd know everything valuable is gone. All I wanted was to build the biggest casino in Las Vegas. I wanted it to be the best. I couldn't raise the money on my own. Then I had several cartel leaders offering every penny I'd ever need. All I had to do was turn this building into a casino and death machine."

Heath broke down into tears. "When I locked this place down, I was out of my mind. I heard that monster outside, and the military, and I thought, well, I thought they were coming for me. I was a fool. They were really after that damn monster outside."

"Enough with the apology," Nick said. "You had no problem murdering my friend, Audra. You knew what would happen when you hit that button. So quit apologizing, asshole."

Heath sneered. The expression caused new blood to ooze from his face. "Fine. Yeah. I knew good people would die. I also knew once the government was onto me, the cartel's promises of my safety were out the window. The cartel won't answer my calls. They won't help me, but I'll be damned if that monster outside destroys this building. I worked hard to create it, and I'll die fighting for it."

Heath leaned over the console. He pressed several keys. Heath opened a menu on the main console. "This is the building's list of outside defenses. I'm entrusting you to use it to save your life, and your lovely friend's. You kill the monster and you get out of here alive."

Heath's eyes were fluttering in the back of his head. He was having a hard time breathing. "One last thing. If you see those security feeds, you'll notice those ugly bug things are making their way up to our position. I'll buy you more time before they get to this level."

Heath issued the system back onto War Mode.

Nick was taken aback by the throng of nasty creatures attacking the stairways. They were chomping down on the dead remains of the bodies on the gaming floor, and picking clean the bones of those strewn on the stairs, or those killed in strange ways in their rooms.

"Whoever created this system is fucked in the head," Nick said. "Why design a building that can kill innocent people like that?"

"Fear," Heath said, coughing up a mouthful of blood. "When this is done, the world will know what the cartel is willing to do to protect their investments. The government will know masses of innocent people will die if anyone interferes with their operation. They had the money, so I had to do what they said. I agreed, because I had no choice. Whatever they wanted, the reasons didn't matter, as long as I got to own and operate my life's dream."

Nick laughed. "Sounds like a load of hot bullshit, and no offense, Red Panda, but no matter how hard the cartel works to scare the government, we're not backing down from anybody. Once you're on America's shit list, we won't rest until we flush you down the crapper in pieces."

"I wash my hands of the cartel," Red Panda said. "I never wanted this for myself. Nobody lives. Everybody dies. What kind of life is that?"

Heath slumped in his chair and dropped his cigar. He bent over with both hands around his belly, moaning in pain. "Kill the monster. Save the building. I don't want my legacy to be reduced to smithereens. Everything else...is done."

When Heath died, he fell forward out of the chair. Nick nudged aside his body, sat in the chair, and stared at the menu Heath had queued up on the security screen. The options on the screen were almost impossible to believe.

"The cartel really wanted to send a message to the world," Red Panda said. "You mess with us, we'll kill you. Strange how the cartel were among those killed tonight."

"He engaged the system at the wrong time," Nick said. "I guess Heath wasn't the right person to be trusted with such a weapon."

Outside, the monster shrieked.

Raaaaaaaaaaaaaaaaaaaatch!

"Looks like we're going to have to fight this thing, or die here trying. Get ready. Shit's going to get crazy." Nick pressed each button on the console.

"All death systems go. Let's see what this bitch of a building can really do!"

The Ravager

Stomping hard, shrieking, and crying out in rage and anger, The Ravager closed in on The Bitterwell Casino. Its feet crunched on burned up, destroyed vehicles, and crushed dead bodies into even more unidentifiable splatter. The beast only wanted to end the noises, and sleep forever in peace. One more building to destroy and it could return home.

Before the beast could bunch up its fists and strike the building, up from the ground, rising from the grass, heat-seeking missiles blasted from cannons. The Ravager didn't see it coming. The missiles struck home, destroying one knee bone, blasting a sizeable hole in its lower abdomen, and taking a bite out of its neck.

The Ravager's globe eyes flickered with a strobe pulse. Redder and redder, the monster's fury couldn't be contained. Machine guns from the top of The Bitterwell Casino began blasting thousands of rounds of ammunition. New turrets sprouted from the ground floor, unleashing a new stream of missile fire.

The beast lost two fingers on one hand, and the other, a hole was blown through the palm. One of its eyes burst in the socket like a squashed tomato. Six hundred gallons of pus and green blood burst from the serrated socket.

"*Raaaaaaaaaaaaaaaaaaaaaaaaaaaar!*"

The beast's damaged hand swiped across the top of the roof, destroying every cannon and weapon. Ravager threw its head back, pushed out its chest, and tensed its body from top to bottom. The blinding neon green aura shot forth from its body full strength. Green energy blasted the ground where the first missiles shot from the grass. Every cannon was decimated. Literally vaporized. Green fires burned around the building. The body of the building was on fire, and those fires were climbing fast to the upper floors.

Nick couldn't believe that missiles were actually firing from cannons. The monster was damaged, but now, they had really pissed it off.

Red Panda was a balled up mess on the floor. "We're going to die. Why keep fighting it? We're not getting out of here alive."

Nick heard scratching outside the door of the security room. He viewed the security screens. Disgusting creatures were bashing at the door, and doing a good job of dismantling it. It wouldn't be long before the monsters would forge through and attack them inside.

He studied the room, and he saw the weapons cabinet beside the bar set up. Heath Bitterwell was living large, Nick thought, but at least he was smart enough to pack some heat when the shit hit the fan.

"Listen, Red Panda, whatever your name is--"

"It's Jamie, okay?"

"Fine, Jamie. I've worked for the government infiltrating threats against the United States for many years. I've murdered countless people. Blood is on my hands, as much as it is on yours. If we can get out of here alive, we can make another go of life. I never wanted to be America's triggerman, and you didn't want to be the cartel's trigger girl, but right now, I need you to step up. Those bug fucks are about to bust through our door and eat us alive. You have to help me blow them away. Even if we die, I refuse to be eaten alive."

The door was on the verge of being lifted from its hinges.

Nick grabbed a riot gun, and a Mossberg pump action.

He got into firing position, waiting for that door to come down.

Jamie stayed on the floor, and kept crying.

The Ravager aimed its closed fists at the casino. It would unleash a torrent of green death that would level The Bitterwell Casino. Before it could unleash that violent surge of energy, from the forty-fourth floor, a set of glass windows retracted into the building. Up from two fake hotel rooms, two new cannons edged out of the openings in the wall. Out fired bursts of tear gas.

Around the building, in the air, walls of blinding white smoke rendered visibility to zero.

The Ravager's green halo flickered out. The monster slashed at empty air, trying to figure out what was happening. With only one eye, the monster was even more helpless in the blinding smoke.

Those same cannons that fired the tear gas now spattered canisters of incendiary flame.

The Ravager's top half was blanketed in flames.

* * *

Nick did his best to steel himself.

The door was yanked back into the hallway. In its place, crab-faced, praying mantis-eyed, mandible clicking, multiple-eyed hybrid insect/reptile creatures fought each other to be the first in line for the buffet.

The riot gun reduced the first row of bugs into squashed pulp.

"I need you, Jamie! You must react to the situation. I'm just like you. Maybe we played on different teams, but we killed people, and we never wanted that kind of a life for ourselves. I was forced into it, and so were you. Now I need you to step up one more time. Come on, Jamie! NOW'S THE TIME!"

When the riot gun ran dry, Nick delivered showers of 12-gauge fire.

There were hundreds of monsters trying to get into the tiny room.

Nick knew he couldn't keep this up for very long.

The Ravager could feel the flames eat into his skin. He gagged on the stench of his own cooking body. The beast flailed, doing everything it could to put out the flames. The monster was in such pain, it couldn't bring back its protective green aura. Its focused was lost. It could only think of one thing: smashing the building until it was reduced to something less than rubble and dust.

A wild burst of Mac-10 fire swept across the row of encroaching monsters. Jamie waved two Mac-10's at the enemies.

That gave Nick the chance to raid the cabinet. He blasted an M-16 until three clips went dry. Bug and crustacean guts were inches high in the room; what was a putrid mix of yellows, reds, and greens. Nick kicked aside a severed-by-bullets ant-head, because it was still clacking its mandible to eat him. Jamie pumped two .357 magnums into a lobster creature with hairy spider legs until its fat thorax burst into hot death jelly. Nick backed that up with Uzis. He hurled wicked shots into the nasty vermin that deserved nothing better than to be squashed under a shoe.

The ugly things kept pushing aside their dead fellows to reach them. The line wouldn't end. Nothing could stop them. Only slow them.

Nick realized one other problem.

There really was no way out of this building, except in a body bag.

Nick and Jamie kept firing at the monsters anyway. It wouldn't be much longer before their gun supply dwindled down to nothing.

Once the bullets stopped, their deaths would begin.

The Ravager punched the east side of the building, turning the fifty-first up to the sixtieth floor into spraying glass and collapsing beams. The sound of smashing glass soothed the pain of the beast's burning skin. Another punch and three more floors caved in. One, two, three more bashing, crashing mean fists connected with The Bitterwell Casino. Ravager craved more and more destruction. One more blow, maybe two, and the beast knew it could flee back to its island home and finally rest.

Just one more punch.

Out of bullets yet again, Nick was lucky to find a case of grenades at the bottom of the gun cabinet. Nick pulled the pin off of one, chucked it into the hallway, and covered his body over Jamie's. The burst caused plated and wet bodies to wet the outside hallway's walls. Fires broke out in the hallway. That bought them little time to decide a plan.

Nick turned to the window in time to see shards of glass fly right at them. The fist decimated the barrier in a split-second.

Outside chilly air blew across their bodies. Jamie was screaming in terror. Nick did his best to be brave. The Ravager's good eye, that brilliant red menacing orb, glared in at them. Its growl rocked the building on its foundation. The monster wanted them dead *real* bad. Nick watched the monster take a step back from the building, rear back its fist, and deliver another five-finger death message.

Fires and ugly monsters behind them, the beast at the other end, Nick knew this would be his dying moment.

He hugged Jamie close.

"We could've made another try at life," Nick said. "I'm sorry I couldn't save you."

Jamie smiled at him. She held Nick's face. "I'm sure we would've turned things around, baby."

She brought him in for a passionate kiss. Jamie forced his hands on her breasts. He reached up under her top for a better feel. Suddenly, nothing else mattered, except their hot mouths pressing desperately against one another.

Nick couldn't lie to himself.

Of the many ways for a man to die, this wasn't so bad.

The Ravager enjoyed human suffering. The sound of it. The way their soft bodies turned to hot blood and guts when they crashed against the pavement. The damaging of tall buildings. The toppling over giant marvels of superior engineering. The Ravager was beginning to crave destruction. Maybe it wouldn't go to sleep after all. The fire along its body was beginning to die down. Seconds later, the fires ran out of fuel and extinguished themselves.

Watching the two people cower from within the building sparked something in the beast. It would keep on reaping destruction forever, it decided, starting with this last building on the strip.

The Ravager cocked back its fist, and shot forth its arm like a spring-loaded device, and unleashed hell.

The chopper appeared out of the dissipating tear gas surrounding the building. It angled towards the beast, getting in real close.

Chopper Dan locked onto its target.

"Found you, asshole! Get ready to die. You're nothing but a five-dollar hooker with a two-fifty rebate. Now stick this in your ear, YOU BIG PIECE OF SHIT!"

Chopper Dan fired a rocket right into the tiny opening at the side of its head. The rocket entered its ear, penetrated its brain, and erupted. He watched in delight as its good eye burst from the impact from within. Both eye sockets were hurling out flames, and the nastiest, thickest, smoking black brain matter.

The Ravager toppled backwards, breaking its spine in fourteen places when landing.

It stayed down for good.

Chopper Dan could die in peace now.

The beast was dead.

More help was on its way. Give it twenty more seconds, he thought, and this place would be canvassed in every form of government and military defense.

He was about to fly away when he saw the two people in The Bitterwell Casino building wave at him for help.

Chopper Dan did his best to hold on. He wasn't sure how much longer he could live. His internal injuries were making every passing second an agony, but damn it, he thought, he had to try to save these people.

Or die trying.

The helicopter flew in real close. There was a short gap between the building and where Nick and Jamie could jump on. The fire was spreading into the security room. The flames pushed them towards the broken wall. Nick knew they were damn lucky. That helicopter had to be the only lifeline in the city.

Jamie was terrified. She wasn't about to jump, and Nick knew it.

Nick only had one choice.

He picked her up into his arms and leaped from the edge of the building.

Nick could only pray they landed safely in the chopper.

Chopper Dan

The din of the media frenzy outside his door woke Chopper Dan in his hospital bed. He couldn't move, except to turn his head when the door opened. He anticipated a wave of nosy reporters drowning him in questions. Who came inside was quite the surprise.

Kathy Ingrid.

Chopper Dan hadn't seen her in many years. His memory of her seemed to be preserved correctly. Kathy hadn't aged a day. She wasn't dressed as a reporter. Kathy was herself. She wore jeans, and a slim-fitting top that exposed a healthy amount of cleavage. Her hair was a dirty blonde, and down to the shoulders; not in a hermetic bun, like on TV. Chopper Dan didn't have to use his imagination, and it was a good thing, because he didn't have the energy. He couldn't help but smile at her.

"'Atta boy," Kathy said. "I know you're going to get better. I talked to Dr. Linwood. She said you've got a nice collection of broken bones, and you've damaged some organs. The doctor assured me with some bed rest, you'll recover."

"Bed rest, huh? So I'm stuck here to enjoy these lovely accommodations?"

"You're lucky to be alive," Kathy said, seriously. "It's...unbelievable. In fact, I would consider what happened a bunch of lies, if it wasn't for you, and the numerous pictures of that beast, and the fact that Las Vegas is pretty much wiped out."

"The monster is dead? Please tell me its dead for good."

Kathy stood over his bed and held his hand. "You killed it. The footage was caught on video. Right when you took that beast down, the Calvary showed up. The military found you had landed your chopper in a nearby parking lot. You weren't conscious."

"I don't remember landing," Chopper Dan admitted. "I was in so much pain, I must've blacked out. I remember shooting a missile, then the damn thing falling down...and then that's it. The rest is a blank."

"You better come up with something more dramatic than that. The media is all over this. You should see how they're having to transport the remains of that gigantic monster. Crews are blowing up chunks of its body with dynamite. Volunteers are loading up semi-trucks with the guts and mess, and whatever the scientists don't take to their labs for study, they're dumping in the ocean. It's quite the scene.

"Other crews are sorting through the wreckage of Las Vegas, and seeking any survivors, gathering up the victims, and cleaning up what's been destroyed...which is pretty much everything. They'll want to talk to you soon."

"I don't want to talk to reporters," Chopper Dan said. "I only wanted to do the right thing...and for you to know I'm very sorry for what happened when I got fired from that news job. The sad thing, I was drunk when I said those things on-air, and the truth is that I have always had the utmost respect for you, and your character. Everything about you is..."

Kathy put her finger on his mouth. "*Shhh*. It's okay. You apologized, and I accept your apology. Can I tell you a secret, Dan?"

"Sure."

"You're divorced, and I'm single. You want to know another statistic? I haven't been laid in three months."

"That's almost a drought," Dan said, smiling. "No life can be sustained in those conditions."

Kathy laughed. "You always had a strange sense of humor. You want to know another secret?"

"Of course."

"The doctor said if we were quiet enough, and we went easy at it, you'd be okay to, uh, you know."

"I'm not sure what you're getting at?"

Kathy locked the door. She shut the blinds.

"Let me put it this way, my big Chopper man. Guess who's not wearing any panties?"

N.A.C.

All the hard work of disappearing off of the face of the earth was behind him. Nick was sitting at the bar in a cheap hotel located in Chihuahua, Mexico, enjoying a beer, and sitting next to Red Panda. She only wanted to be called Jamie, so Nick respected her wishes. They were both new people now. Nick was working on getting them legit identification. That would take time, and pulling the right connections, and being careful every step of the way. The government would want their toy soldier back. The cartel probably felt the same way about Jamie. Nick prayed one factor would help their cause of vanishing themselves off of the face of the planet.

People would assume they were both dead.

Las Vegas was in ruins. Nick watched the news. The media was covering up the fact The Bitterwell Casino was a maze of death. Anything about the cartel's involvement about the casino was kept quiet. Total media blackout. What couldn't be contained was the giant beast. There was no denying its existence. What the world would ultimately do with that information was still yet to be determined.

Nick was enjoying a conversation with Jamie about the things they could do with their lives now that they weren't trapped anymore by the government and the cartel.

The bartender served them each a shot of bourbon.

The Mexican bartender said in rough English that the gentleman in the corner purchased them the drinks. The man was in his late fifties, wearing a pair of green fatigue pants and a tight black muscle shirt. The stranger invited himself over. He sat in the stool next to them.

"The name's James Garfield."

James shook their hand.

Nick's heckles were raised. "You're a government goon, aren't you? How you found us, I don't even know."

"I'm not a government goon," James said, raising up his shot glass and firing it down the hatch. "I'm actually a part of an organization that's been created because of government fuck-ups. Yeah, I work for the United States, but I'm my own goon, and I take care of tasks that I see fit to tackle. Nobody tells me what to do. Those who work with me understand the importance of their missions. We don't do cover-ups, or bullshit politics."

Nick still wasn't impressed. "Then what is it that you do, and what does that have to do with us?"

"That monster attack you survived in Las Vegas," James replied, "was something the United States government was watching, and yes, they did stick you in there not as a vacation, but as a way to smoke out Heath Bitterwell, and his cartel dealings. I'm sure you know a little bit about that, Jamie Blevins. Or should I call you...Red Panda?"

"Don't threaten me, and don't threaten her," Nick said. "I'll drive your face into this counter. I don't know how you found me so fast. Damn you, people. I'm so sick of being used for killing. I can't do it anymore."

James didn't appear to be phased by the threats. "Here's the deal. The government will keep hounding you. They'll either put you to work, lock you up, or bury you in the system. I'm your best option."

"Oh yeah? Is that right, James Garfield? You here to improve my standard of living? So far, my life's been a standard of dying. The problem, I can't die. I should've died in Vegas. Death doesn't stop following me. Every where I go, there's another pile of dead bodies."

"Stop feeling sorry for yourself," James said, ordering another round of shots. "I'm not a government goon. I'm connected with them, sure, and we share information, and we work together, but my work is very...specific. It'd be a nice change of pace for you, Nick.

"And you, Jamie, you're facing a long list of murder charges, drug possession, conspiracy, and a long ass laundry list of felonies.

Consider yourself locked up in maximum-security prison for the rest of your life, and your pretty ass, you'd be fresh meat. They like 'em cute in prison, and you, girl, are real cute.

"Keep staring at me, Nick. You're about to charge at me like a bull. Think for a minute. Drop the angry, bad boy, psychologically damaged act. I know about your parents in Afghanistan. I know how Uncle Sam turned you into a killing machine. I can help you get treatment. I got a team of therapists who will really help you. Your life will get better, if you let me help you. The both of you."

Nick knew many operatives who could sell snake oil and bullshit like the best of them. There was always a price, and he was the one who had to pay it.

Nick decided to find out what the fuck this guy actually wanted.

"What's the assignment, pal? Get on with it. What the hell are you throwing us into?"

"In exchange for your total allegiance to our program, what we call the New American Coalition, N.A.C., for short, I'll get you the psychological help you need, Nick, and Jamie, I can wipe your record clean. If I do that, you work for me. You do as I say, throw yourself in harm's way, and you don't expect me to explain why, or to wipe your ass clean and your face dry of tears when the shit gets real."

"Who am I killing?" Nick insisted. He was getting antsy. "Just tell me the details."

"It's not *who* you're killing, Nick," James said, "it's *what*. You and your friend survived Las Vegas. We know about the other monsters you fought off at The Bitterwell Casino. Well, there are threats popping up across the world just like them. Monsters. Sea beasts. Impossible enemies. N.A.C. dispatches them, and you'll be joining us if you agree to help us. That's the job.

"The thing is, our government, the one who fucks up everything, has an underground bunker in Arizona. They've locked up hundreds of these monsters over many decades. The problem, a band of terrorists have taken it hostage. They're threatening to release these monsters upon the world if we don't answer to their terms. We have to re-take the facility, dispatch the terrorists, and prevent the monsters from escaping.

"I've got a nice elite team put together, and I want to add you to the roster. If you agree, we go to work immediately. So you can join us, or you'll be arrested, Jamie, and you, Nick, will go back to work as the government's bitch. What's your play, guys?"

Jamie gave Nick a troubled expression.

Nick put his hands into Jamie's.

"We'll both be together on this team, correct?"

"Yes, you'll be working together."

"I won't leave you," Nick told Jamie. "We're in this together. Looks like we don't have much of a choice."

James smiled, and toasted them with a new round of shots. "So you're in?"

"Yeah, I suppose so. Looks like I'm fucked in any direction I turn." Nick toasted to Jamie and James. "To us. Newly minted monster killers. Sounds like the change of pace we need. We'll blow the fuck out of whatever comes our way."

The three drank to blowing the fuck out of whatever came their way.

 SEVERED**PRESS**

 facebook.com/severedpress
 twitter.com/severedpress

CHECK OUT OTHER GREAT KAIJU NOVELS

KAIJU WINTER
by Jake Bible

The Yellowstone super volcano has begun to erupt, sending North America into chaos and the rest of the world into panic. People are dangerous and desperate to escape the oncoming mega-eruption, knowing it will plunge the continent, and the world, into a perpetual ashen winter. But no matter how ready humanity is, nothing can prepare them for what comes out of the ash: Kaiju!

RAIJU
by K.H. Koehler

His home destroyed by a rampaging kaiju, Kevin Takahashi and his father relocate to New York City where Kevin hopes the nightmare is over. Soon after his arrival in the Big Apple, a new kaiju emerges. Qilin is so powerful that even the U.S. Military may be unable to contain or destroy the monster. But Kevin is more than a ragged refugee from the now defunct city of San Francisco. He's also a Keeper who can summon ancient, demonic god-beasts to do battle for him, and his creature to call is Raiju, the oldest of the ancient Kami. Kevin has only a short time to save the city of New York. Because Raiju and Qilin are about to clash, and after the dust settles, there may be no home left for any of them!

SEVEREDPRESS

 facebook.com/severedpress
 twitter.com/severedpress

CHECK OUT OTHER GREAT KAIJU NOVELS

MURDER WORLD I KAIJU DAWN
by Jason Cordova
& Eric S Brown

Captain Vincente Huerta and the crew of the Fancy have been hired to retrieve a valuable item from a downed research vessel at the edge of the enemy's space.
It was going to be an easy payday.
But what Captain Huerta and the men, women and alien under his command didn't know was that they were being sent to the most dangerous planet in the galaxy.
Something large, ancient and most assuredly evil resides on the planet of Gorgon IV. Something so terrifying that man could barely fathom it with his puny mind. Captain Huerta must use every trick in the book, and possibly write an entirely new one, if he wants to escape Murder World.

KAIJU ARMAGEDDON
by Eric S. Brown

The attacks began without warning. Civilian and Military vessels alike simply vanished upon the waves. Crypto-zoologist Jerry Bryson found himself swept up into the chaos as the world discovered that the legendary beasts known as Kaiju are very real. Armies of the great beasts arose from the oceans and burrowed their way free of the Earth to declare war upon mankind. Now Dr. Bryson may be the human race's last hope in stopping the Kaiju from bringing civilization to its knees.
This is not some far distant future. This is not some alien world. This is the Earth, here and now, as we know it today, faced with the greatest threat its ever known. The Kaiju Armageddon has begun.

www.ingramcontent.com/pod-product-compliance
Lightning Source LLC
Chambersburg PA
CBHW051959170626
46808CB00007B/2688